A shadowy mist had cr[illegible]
gaunt corpses of trees looke[illegible]
seemed to move in slow motion. Johnny whistled a
tune—or tried to. The air grew chilly, curling around his ears.

He clenched his teeth and lifted his taut chin high. Then he shouted: "I'M JOHNNY ELBERT FINLAY, PROTECTOR OF WILD LIFE!" Lowering his voice, he stammered, "N-nothin' on this here mountain scares m-me."

Johnny stopped. There was no breeze. Out of the silent shadows, he was sure he heard something—rustling, or scraping not far behind him. Or was it just the pounding of his heart? . . .

COURAGE on MIRROR MOUNTAIN

COURAGE on MIRROR MOUNTAIN

WYNNETTE FRASER

A White Horse Book
Published by Chariot Books™
an imprint of David C. Cook Publishing Co.
David C. Cook Publishing Co., Elgin, Illinois 60120
David C. Cook Publishing Co., Weston, Ontario

Cover design by Starry Night Studio
Cover illustration by Jeffrey R. Busch
Edited by Dave and Neta Jackson

First printing, 1989
Printed in the United States of America
93 92 91 90 89 5 4 3 2 1

Library of Congress Cataloging-in-Publication Data

Fraser, Wynnette, 1925-
Courage on Mirror Mountain/Wynnette Fraser.
p. cm.
Summary: A young boy living in the mountains of South Carolina grows in courage, understanding, and responsibility when he helps an injured hawk return to the wild.
[1. Hawks—Fiction. 2. Mountain life—Fiction.
3. Christian life—Fiction.]
I. Title.
PZ7.F8643Co 1989 [Fic]—dc19 89-31978
ISBN 1-55513-039-9 CIP AC

To my grandchildren:
Scott McRee, Matt McRee
Bryan Fraser, and Casey Fraser

With thanks to Kent Nickerson, master falconer,
Columbia, South Carolina,
for information on hawks.

Contents

Louise's Song

People don't have wings
Like birds and pretty angels do,
But my Jesus brings me
A song I can sing, so
He's taught me a way to fly, too.

Chorus:
In my heart I have wings—
Wings to soar where He sends me;
My spirit goes higher than I'll ever fly,
For His love, joy, and peace are within me.
Wings! In my heart I have wings. . .

Sometimes skies are gray
And thermals don't move high;
But the sun shines again, so
I look for a rainbow
And get myself ready to fly.

1
Something Eerie

"Next time we camp out, let's not fix pancakes or anything that takes so much cleanup!" declared Johnny Finlay.

Scott Jenkins looked at his watch. "I agree. It took us a full hour to get the soot off your mother's iron skillet. I was counting on looking for arrowheads before going to watch the hang gliders at Mirror Rock."

"We've still got time," Johnny assured him, tossing his head to shake a shock of light brown hair from his forehead. "I'm just glad you brought paper plates and spoons. It's a lot easier chucking them into the fire than washing more dishes." The coals made a hissing sound as he poured water on them to put out the fire.

Scott added handfuls of sand till no more smoke rose from the ashes. "I might be a Cub Scout, but who needs to waste time washing dishes?"

"Not me," answered Johnny.

It was ten o'clock on a clear Saturday morning, and spring was apple-green on Mirror Mountain. Tiny leaves unfolded to catch the heat and light. Forest creatures crept, crawled, and slithered; bird noises rode the sun-drenched air. A few feet away from the boys, Way-High Creek licked at its rocky banks.

The two boys had slept till nearly eight, built a fire and cooked breakfast for themselves. Now, Johnny's hazel eyes moved over the rolled-up sleeping bags, knapsacks and food cooler.

"Sandy said for us to just leave our stuff on the back deck of the church," he said. "We ain't to disturb him while he's workin' on his sermon. We can put the gear in the storeroom later."

Beyond a pine-covered slope, one tall gable rose between two chimneys that flanked the Church on the Mountain. Last fall, Johnny's Uncle Elbert had donated the use of his vacant log cabin for indoor meetings. Sandy McRee, a ministerial student at Cougarville College, lived there. Each day he drove Johnny and his sister, Louise, down the steep and twisted mountain road to school. From the base of the mountain, it was five miles to Cougarville Elementary. After leaving the children there, Sandy drove to college for his classes.

At last the camping gear was ready to go. But Scott

pointed to a pint jar labelled, "Earle Finlay's Sourwood Honey." It was three-fourths full. "What about that?" he asked. "There's no room left in the cooler."

Johnny twisted his wide mouth while his brain worked on the problem. They couldn't leave that much for the ants. "We'll hang it on a limb," he decided. With his pocket knife, he cut some fish line from a spool. One end of the line was tied around the jar's neck, the other about a rough stone. While Scott held on to the jar, Johnny tossed the stone over a dogwood limb twice. Securely balanced by the weight of the stone, the golden honey glowed from bits of sunlight that trickled through the leaves.

"Won't the ants still come down that line?" Scott wondered.

"Not when I'm through." Johnny found a tube of petroleum jelly that his mother had sent along for cuts and scrapes. He spread big globs of it on the line above the jar. "That'll fix them thievin' little critters," he said.

"You know how to do everything," Scott marveled. "We could use you in my Scout troop."

"I'm too old to start Cub Scouts," eleven-year-old Johnny said.

Scott looked apologetic. Both boys knew the little Finlay house was too far up the mountain road for Johnny to get to after-school activities.

Many people thought it odd that the son of the wealthy owner of Cougarville Textiles was best-friends with Johnny Finlay. The big Jenkins home had wide, well-kept lawns and a swimming pool that Scott often enjoyed. The Finlays, on the other hand, were just mountain people who got by the best they could. But nine-year-old Scott Jenkins loved roaming over the mountain to collect Indian relics. And Johnny knew where such treasures would be uncovered whenever it rained on Mirror Mountain.

The two boys had become good friends, but nothing completely erased Johnny's awareness of the years that stood between them. He wished he could do something with boys his own age.

"I might play on Ray Arthur's baseball team next year," he shared casually. Ray Arthur, Johnny's redheaded cousin, was thirteen, mischievous and fun-loving. "The county's fixin' the road up this here mountain, and Pa might get a car. I could ride home with him after practice."

"Great!" approved Scott with sincerity as they reached the back of the church and eased their bundles down quietly onto the wooden deck.

After strapping on their knapsacks, they walked a big log that lay across the creek and then took the trail that held to the mountain top. There they would find Mirror Rock, the large granite outcropping from which Mirror Mountain got its name.

From time to time, Scott picked up a rock to examine. If he decided it would be a good addition to his collection, it went into his knapsack. If not, it was discarded.

They reached the spot where two forestry students from Jimson College had planted trees last summer.

"What time do the hang gliders usually get to Mirror Rock?" Scott asked, glancing at his watch.

"When the sun's good and high," said Johnny. "The air currents aren't right for them until it's warm. But we'll hear their Jeeps driving up the mountain before then. Them grinders complain all the way up."

Johnny pointed with pride to the little trees. Tiny buds had appeared on them. "I been lookin' after 'em," he said, "so's they won't die like so many trees up here been doin'. Hank and Rusty'll soon be back again."

"I know," Scott said. "This summer, Dad's company is sponsoring their reforestry project."

"I'm gonna be one some day."

"One what?"

"You know, one of them people who saves plants and wild life."

"A conservationist?" asked Scott.

"That's it." Johnny put his hands on his hips and heaved an impatient sigh. He never seemed to be able to remember that name.

Scott moved over to the east side of the trail. He peeped through bony trees to a formation of large granite boulders. "We've never been to that part of the mountain," he said.

"Reckon not. That's where the hermit hut is."

"A hermit lives there?"

"No, but they say his ghost does. Hermit Dan died of a heart attack two years back. The path starts long about here. It's all covered up now."

Scott's brown eyes were bright with excitement. "A

ghost on Mirror Mountain! Just think of that." He glanced at Johnny, as if trying to see his thoughts. "Of course, I really don't believe in ghosts," he added guardedly.

"Mmmm," Johnny murmured. "It's just hearsay. I've never been down there, myself. Guess it's 'cause I was always taught to leave old Hermit Dan alone when he was living."

"Are you scared of ghosts?"

"Me? No way! You might say I'm a mite respectful, though—like at a wake or funeral." Johnny's hazel eyes took on a mischievous glint. He lowered his voice to a ghoulish, eerie whisper. "They say Dan's ghost walks Top Trail at night. He might even be around in daylight—you can feel it in the air, or hear him in the bushes."

"Shhh!" whispered Scott, his eyes wider than ever. "I feel cold, and the air is stiller than I've ever felt."

Johnny realized it was true. Chill bumps stood out on his short arms. His heart picked up speed—at least it seemed that way. In the bushes near the trail, they heard a rustling sound. They went into a huddle, unable to take their eyes from a clump of laurel bushes as the sound continued.

Then suddenly the brush parted, and a long, dark nose appeared. It was followed by the rest of a big, black dog. Its tail wagged nonstop as the animal bounded up to the boys and jumped up on them.

"Midnight!" Scott cried as he joyfully hugged the animal. "We thought you were a ghost, for sure!" Aunt

Lou Finlay's dog never failed to track down Johnny, wherever he went on the mountain.

They laughed with relief as the air seemed to be filled with warmth and brightness once more.

"We might as well go check out the hermit hut now," Johnny decided with a grin. "After all, we got the Mighty Midnight to protect us."

Johnny led the way around the head-high rocks that for years had hid the path to the old hut from outsiders who might not have respected the hermit's privacy.

2
The Hermit Hut

As far back as Johnny could remember, Hermit Dan and his goats had been a part of the mountain. Dan's private domain, however, was separated from other people by the cluster of tall boulders. Top Trail hikers couldn't see what the boulders hid, and mountain people respected the boundary they marked. If Dan needed their help, he knew where to look for them, but he seldom asked for any.

"What did he look like?" Scott asked as they thrashed through the tall weeds that had overgrown the path.

"He was a head taller than Pa, but not chunky like him," recalled Johnny. "His clothes hung loose, and he had a beard. It was gray and bushy. His hair was long and flyin' in the wind."

"Sounds like a wild man," said Scott.

"I reckon so, but his eyes wasn't wild at all. They had a gentle, sad look in 'em." He paused, then added, "I saw him at Aunt Lou's sometimes. He'd come there for staple goods."

"Your Aunt Lou gave him food?"

"Didn't give. Dan was too proud for that. He'd trade wild herbs for flour and sugar—stuff like that."

"What'd he eat?"

"Guess he drank goat's milk and ate wild plants. Maybe he ate a goat now 'n then, to thin out his herd."

They plodded on through tangles of weeds and vines. Johnny told Scott what he could remember about the hermit's death. It had been cold, below freezing for days. Dan had told Aunt Lou to expect him on February 15. She knew she could count on him coming exactly when he said he would. So when he didn't, Aunt Lou had one of her "peculiar" feelings that something was wrong.

So she sent Pa to check on him, and he found Dan's body. When the coroner checked him, he said Dan had been dead for two days. There was nothing in the hut to reveal Dan's last name, or where to look for relatives. Aunt Lou said she knew the old hermit had a Bible. She thought it might have his name in it, but no one could find it.

"You mean there wasn't even a funeral?" Scott asked.

"Oh, yeah; there was a funeral. Aunt Lou wouldn't have it no other way," said Johnny as he kicked a stone with the toe of his sneaker. "Some of the men built a pine coffin, and he was buried over in the mountain cemetery. Uncle Elbert read the Twenty-third Psalm and they sang 'Abide With Me.'

"What happened to the goats?"

"Mr. Lonnie Shook found homes for 'em."

Midnight had left the boys to chase a rabbit by the time they reached the tall boulders. Cautiously, the boys crept around them and found themselves on a wide, rock-strewn ledge. Against the other side of the granite formation stood the hermit hut, its one small window veiled with dust. Beside the hut was another smaller building with no windows at all.

"Those buildings look like they're stuck to the mountainside," observed Scott.

"I'd say more like they was blown there by the wind." Johnny's sharp hazel eyes took in the odd mixture of junk materials that had been used in constructing the place: old license plates, tin, warped plywood, and roofing scraps. A rusty screen door hung askew over a wooden one. On it, strips of peeled gray paint lay in curls. A small hole was chiseled through both doors at the bottom.

When he tried it, the lock pulled apart in Johnny's hand. "It was just set to look fastened," he told Scott.

With a loud squawk, the door swung opened. A musty smell rose to greet them. As he let his eyes adjust to the dim light, a little shiver ran over Johnny. He hoped Scott hadn't noticed, but the younger boy was busy propping both doors open with a rock.

With a sigh of relief, Johnny was glad to see no shadowy figures lurking in the bright light that now filled the room. Above them, several bunches of decayed herbs, laced with cobwebs, were strung from the rafters.

"I see why Dan built the hut against rock," Johnny said. "He didn't need to put up but three sides. See how the rafters was laid on them rock outcroppings?"

"Neat idea," observed Scott. "The roof's just a bit lopsided, though."

A big wooden box stood on its side against one wall. A zinc bucket with a gourd dipper sat on top of the box in a speckled basin. Underneath were several rusty lard tins.

Near the window, in a hole cut to size, a short joint of stove pipe remained. At some time, there must have been a stove that attached to it.

The only thing that might be called furniture was a shabby cot. Its mattress was bare of linens, and yellowed cotton spilled out of holes in its faded, blue-striped cover.

"Rats done that," Johnny pointed out. "That mattress is bound to be crawlin' with 'em."

"Looks like nobody's been here for a long time," Scott said. "When a place in town gets vacant, vandals come and tear it up."

"Well, somebody's gone through this place with a fine-tooth comb since Dan died, too, 'cause ain't nothin' left worth having." He kicked aside a pile of old papers and rubbish, thinking of the Bible Aunt Lou was sure existed, but it wasn't there.

When they were outside again, Scott moved the rock and Johnny closed both doors, fixing the lock just as it had been before.

They looked at the windowless building. Its door was about four feet high, and its latch was a crude wooden one.

Remembering the days before Pa had installed indoor plumbing, Johnny said, "What a funny looking outhouse."

Scott turned the latch and pulled a chain that was nailed above it. Nothing happened.

"It must be stuck," Johnny said. "Let me help you." After several forceful tugs, the rain-swollen door popped open and sent them in a backward tumble.

"Why, it's bright as day in there!" Scott exclaimed as they scrambled over each other for a look.

"That's 'cause there ain't no roof," concluded Johnny. "All the roof it's got is just some old tree limbs laid criss-cross like bars."

"Why would that be?" Scott wondered. "What a strange man Hermit Dan must've been."

" 'Strange' might be the right word," agreed Johnny. "Anyhow, it sure ain't no privy. There's no toilet hole, just that flat board sittin' on the ground in the middle."

"And some kind of post in the corner," Scott added. "It looks like a cross. Maybe this was his prayer room!"

"Uh-huh. And maybe he kneeled on the board. I'd've prayed outside if it was me."

They backed out, fastened the latch, and went to

the brink of the ledge. Down a straight drop of about ten feet, another narrower ledge dropped sharply a few feet more into a massive briar thicket. The briar patch cloaked the next hundred feet of the mountainside. On the other side, its thorny runners pointed like fingers to a green field with a little brook that snaked through it. The meadow sloped a long distance to some trees that hid the long road that came around from the north side of the mountain. The slope was surrounded by tall trees on either side.

They found some crude steps that led to the lower ledge. They were built of small rocks, and baby leaves of Virginia Creeper peeped from between the chinks.

Scott turned and looked at the hut once more. "What a neat place this would be for a club to meet!" he exclaimed. "If we just had one or two more guys to start one!"

"Shhhh," Johnny held up a hand and cocked his head, listening. "I hear Midnight. He's all shook up about something!"

3
Charley Hawk

Midnight's bark had a loud, persistent ring to it and came from the other side of the granite boulders.

They found the dog beside a narrow ravine about eight feet deep. Jagged rocks studded the bank on each side. At the bottom, a big bird repeatedly lifted only one broad wing. And each time it did so, the bird tumbled over awkwardly. "It's a red-tailed hawk!" Johnny exclaimed. "Something's wrong with one of its wings."

Midnight kept on bawling. The frightened bird vainly struggled to pull itself to a take-off position.

"Quiet!" Johnny ordered. He gave the dog a firm slap across its butt. Still snorting and whining, Midnight stood back.

"Can we get the hawk out of there?" Scott asked.

"Not by ourselves. We need help."

"But who?"

Johnny thought a moment, then brightened. "Sandy! He told me he worked with hawks when he was a teenager. He'll know what to do!"

The sound of Jeep motors had grown loud enough for the boys to know that the hang glider pilots would soon be up on Mirror Rock, assembling their big kites, and ready to launch very soon.

"Guess we won't see them today," Scott said, looking disappointed.

"We'll catch 'em next time," Johnny consoled. "But if I'm gonna be a conservationist, I have to try 'n save that hawk."

After running back down to the church, they found Sandy in the kitchen. He was wearing jeans and a comfortable looking faded polo shirt. A wonderful steamy aroma filled the room.

"You're just in time to try my homemade vegetable soup," he told them with a relaxed smile. On the table was an electric Crockpot.

Johnny's impatience was racing inside of him. "Thanks, but we ain't got time now," he said with regret. Hurriedly, he gave the details of the injured hawk.

Sandy listened with interest. "From what you've told me, it doesn't sound too serious," he said. Then he placed a steadying hand on Johnny's shoulder. "A few more minutes won't matter."

Out of the cabinet came a jar of peanut butter,

which the young man plunked down in front of the boys. Then he pointed to a box of Saltines. "While you're eating, I'll go round up some things I think we'll need for the rescue."

"I won't argue," clipped Scott, helping himself to a hefty bowl of soup.

It made Johnny hungry just smelling it. "Maybe I'll have a little bowl of that, after all," he said as he took the soup ladle from his friend.

Before the rescue trio left, they locked Midnight in the church storeroom with a few soothing words and a very tasty soup bone.

Sandy had with him a pair of heavy gloves and a large, old sock. He had cut the toe out of it. Scott carried a plastic bag with raw hamburger in it, and Johnny carried a small, leather, hawk's hood in his hand.

When they got back to the ravine, the hawk was in almost the same place they had last seen it. Only now it rested on leaves that had collected in the chasm. But the bird's bright eyes were open and watchful.

Sandy put on the gloves. He used the jagged rocks as footholds to climb down the embankment. As he approached, the hawk began to flail about again. Speaking softly, he quickly grasped its ankles just above the sharp talons. In a flash, the hawk was slipped into the sock, head first. Its head looked funny sticking out of the hole in the toe of the sock. Next, Sandy slid the leather hood over the bird's head. With one end of the drawstrings in his teeth, he gently secured the ties around its neck.

With open mouths, Scott and Johnny had watched from above. Sandy glanced up now. An amused smile crossed his handsome face as he noticed their puzzled looks.

"The hood is used to keep him calm—so things he might see don't frighten him," he explained. "In case you're interested, he's a male."

The two boys continued to kneel as if they were glued to the spot. The hawk looked strange in the white sock, with the hood hiding its piercing eyes.

"I always wondered why I brought this old hood up here with me," Sandy mused. "Now I'll have to hand him up to one of you guys so I can climb out of here."

Johnny looked at Scott, who shook his head. Then he looked down at Sandy, whose eyes were bright and amused.

So Sandy didn't think he had the nerve to handle a hawk! *Well, I'll show him*, thought Johnny. He took a deep breath, then reached down.

"I-I'll take him," he managed to stammer. His hands quivered as they closed around the funny bundle. The heat from the bird's body could be felt through the sock. As quickly as it had come, the scared feeling went away.

Sandy pulled himself from the ravine and took the hawk from Johnny. He removed the sock and examined the injured wing. "Just as I thought," he said. "It's only sprained."

"But, Sandy—hawks have to catch food to live,"

Johnny reminded him, "and this one can't fly."

"You're right," Sandy agreed. "We need a safe place to keep him till the wing heals. That means we'll have to feed him ourselves for several weeks."

"Maybe we could build a cage," Scott suggested. Sandy shook his head. "Never cage a hawk! He's likely to die sooner than if we left him where we found him. What we need is a hawk loft. My dad helped me build one for a hawk I trained when I was fifteen. It's just a small room without windows and no top—except for bamboo poles laid over it to let in air and sunlight."

The boys looked at each other in surprise.

"So that's what it was!" exclaimed Scott.

Johnny nodded agreement. "For sure, it wasn't no prayer room."

Sandy cast a puzzled glance at the boys. "What in the world are you boys talking about?"

"The hawk loft! We've already found one," Scott cried.

"Hermit Dan must have kept a hawk," Johnny explained, "'cause a room like you said is right by his hut. It's around them big rocks there. Come on, we'll show you."

It was nothing short of a miracle, they agreed. The loft had been discovered just in time for the injured hawk to move in.

"We ought to check this out with your father," Sandy told Johnny. "We want to be sure we're not trespassing on private property."

The boys learned that the wooden "cross" in the loft

was actually a perch for a hawk to sit on.

"That one good wing will get him on and off the perch," assured Sandy.

"What will we name him?" Scott asked.

Sandy scratched his head. "I don't want you guys to get too attached to him. This state has laws against keeping birds of prey in captivity."

"I don't want to keep him after he can fly again," said Johnny. "But I'd like to have something to call him in the meantime."

"Fine," Sandy agreed. While they went over a lot of names, Sandy put the hawk on his perch and took off the leather hood. Gently, the bird swayed from side to side. His sharp eyes scanned every corner of the airy little room. The feathers on his wings lay in perfectly balanced waves. Shafts of sunlight slid through the loft top enriching the colors: rust, ivory and light brown.

"Let's just call him 'Charley,'" suggested Johnny.

"Charley Hawk," Scott said. "Once my Dad had a stiff muscle, and he called it a 'charley horse.' Guess a sprain's something like that for a hawk."

"He ain't gonna want to be reminded of his stupid accident," Johnny said. "I just thought 'Charley' would suit him."

Scott readily agreed. "It's an easy name to say."

"Well, now that you've got that settled, I think Charley may be glad for some food," Sandy said as he backed up to the door.

Scott and Johnny had not yet come inside the loft.

While Sandy introduced Charley to his new quarters, the two boys had waited outside and peeped through the cracked door.

"I want Charley to get used to you while I'm here," Sandy told them. He pointed to the bag of meat that was still in Scott's hand. "Both of you go inside and walk slowly to the feeding board. Then open and dump the hamburger meat on it. I'll wait here and watch."

Johnny didn't want to be scared. He didn't want Scott to know he was uneasy about this ordeal. But he could see his own feelings surfacing in the younger boy. "Come on, man," he beckoned.

They crept slowly toward the board. All at once, the big bird rose as tall as he could. He flared out his beautiful body feathers. Then he raised the crest on his head and glared boldly at them. The boys paused, not wanting to go on.

"Put down the meat and leave!" Sandy ordered firmly. "He won't attack. He's just acting defensive."

Not at all sure Sandy was right, they hurriedly obeyed. All the time, they cast cautious glances at Charley. After backing out, they watched through the crack. Charley glided down lopsidedly and began to devour the meat.

"It's gonna take a lot of raw meat to feed him," worried Johnny as he latched the door.

"I can get meat scraps from the supermarket," Scott offered, "and bring them to you at school. I've got a cooler that ought to fit in a school locker."

"That's great, but there's one hitch," said Sandy. "You can't feed just meat by itself to a bird of prey."

"Huh?" questioned Johnny.

"Charley needs a certain amount of fur or feathers in his diet to stay healthy."

"Ugh!" Scott made a face. "You mean they swallow that stuff?"

"Not exactly. The fur and feathers roll up in balls that clean the hawk's crop. It's like cleaning a bottle with a brush."

"If he don't swallow it, where does it go?" asked Johnny.

Sandy gazed at the view from the ledge. "Every morning, the bird throws up the ball of fur and feathers. It's called 'casting.'"

"So where will we get fur and feathers?" Scott wondered.

"Set rat traps. Charley's going to need five or six rats per day. Meat scraps are okay about twice a week."

"I'll set traps in Aunt Lou's barn," Johnny said.

"And I'll set them in the church storeroom," Sandy said. "We'll take turns. If you'll feed him tomorrow, I'll be responsible on Monday."

"All right," agreed Johnny, "only don't nobody tell Aunt Lou we're helpin' a hawk. She's out to kill 'em for stealing her chickens!"

Sandy nodded and glanced at his watch, grinning. "I'm going to leave for Cougarville in about an hour," he told Scott. "Will you be ready?"

"Sure," Scott answered.

They walked with Sandy as far as Way-High Creek. There, the boys filled the zinc bucket with water and lugged it back to the ledge. They emptied it into the speckled basin, which they then set inside the loft. This time Charley raised his crest. The boys didn't stay to watch feathers flare or razor eyes fixed on them. They ducked out and latched the door.

Back at the church, they put the leftover honey in Sandy's refrigerator for him to use. Then they let Midnight out of the storeroom. The dog sprinted alongside the yellow, four-wheel-drive station wagon that doubled as a school bus all the way to Johnny's house. The dog didn't stop, but kept running till he got to Aunt Lou's cabin. Midnight did not like to be locked up.

While Louise and Ma washed supper dishes, Johnny and Pa went outside. Johnny liked to sit under the chestnut oak on a bent willow couch his parents had built there.

Pa was interested in hearing about Charley, and promised to ease Sandy's mind about trespassing laws on the mountain. "But we won't tell the womenfolk just yet. You were right. To Aunt Lou, the only good hawk's a dead one!"

They planned to sneak up to the hermit hut before Sunday school the next morning. Pa wanted to see Charley.

4
Wings and Furry Things

When the weather was right, Mirror Rock was proclaimed by hang glider pilots as the best takeoff place in the three upcountry counties of the state. It bellied out from the mountain, turning under itself. About a mile down and over was Jones Meadow where vehicles waited to pick up the pilots after they landed.

When church and the picnic that followed were over, Johnny and his cousin, Ray Arthur, walked behind their fathers to the rock. Uncle Elbert walked tall with a steady, deliberate gait, but Pa almost jogged alongside his taller brother, his head bobbing with excitement. Pa was like a three-year-old at Christmas when he went to watch the hang gliders—and he watched them every chance he got.

Today, Matt Bryan's wife, Casey, drove the four-wheel-drive Jeep. Two of Matt's students were with him. The men's folded hang gliders rode in oblong bags strapped to the top. Each end extended beyond the length of the Jeep.

When the four Finlays arrived at Mirror Rock, the big kites had already been unpacked. They looked like giant butterflies in pastel colors of blue, green, and yellow. Little breezes flitted around them, causing tilts and wobbles.

Matt and Casey waved a greeting to the Finlays. They were too busy to talk with them just then.

Only Matt's advanced students launched themselves off Mirror Rock. Beginners practiced at Cub Point. That was a little hill that overlooked Cougarville College Athletic Field. It was a safe place for new students to "crunch," Matt had told Johnny one day. The instructor was about thirty, not tall, but muscular. When he grinned, everyone of his oversized teeth showed.

Johnny had learned that "crunch" was hang gliding lingo for "crash."

"Accidents are always possible when we go out there," Matt had said in a serious voice. "Before I bring a kiter to launch from Mirror Rock, he has to prove he can handle unexpected air currents." He narrowed his eyes. "Above all, I have to be sure he's not a show-off."

Johnny now stared at the sky beyond the rock. He shaded his eyes against the bright sunlight.

"Look at that pair of red-tails flying," Ray Arthur noted.

The hawks glided smoothly beneath some cumulus clouds that reminded Johnny of Ma's fresh-washed sheets blowing on the line. The warm south breeze lifted a shock of his hair that always fell across his wide forehead. There was no doubt about it. The day was perfect for hang gliding.

Casey Bryan acted as launch assistant. She helped each pilot steady his kite and get strapped into his harness. After briefing the men, Matt pushed off first. He caught the same thermal the hawks were riding. The other kiters followed in the same pattern.

Casey stayed to watch with the Finlays as currents of air lifted the big kites high above the countryside. They looked like sailboats drifting on a blue sea.

"So easy!" marveled Ray Arthur. "Oh no," Casey objected. She pushed her long, dark hair from her face. "Each kiter has to stay alert at all times to correct any kind of problem in air movements," she said. "A sudden change in the air pattern can cause an altitude drop in seconds."

"I reckon you can't tell which way the wind's gonna blow," agreed Johnny.

"Air acts like water does," Casey went on. "Isn't there a rocky creek running down the mountain over yonder?"

Johnny nodded. "We call it Way-High Creek," he said. "Sometimes it runs smooth. But when it hits rocks, it goes all kinds of ways."

"It's the same with air currents," Casey told him. "It depends on what's in the way—"

"Like rocks and trees and hills," Ray Arthur put in. Casey smiled at him and nodded in agreement.

It was a pretty sight, thought Johnny; hang gliders and hawks riding the same warm streams of air. How nice it must be just to take off and float above all cares. Yet Casey had just pointed out that hang gliding had lots of dangers to watch for. Hawks had their troubles, too. Hadn't Charley been grounded by a sprained wing? No, he decided. It wasn't simple, not at all.

Casey left to drive down to Jones Meadow to pick up the hang gliders. But the Finlays kept watching the gliders dip and dive beneath puffy clouds.

"I'm gonna do that myself," announced Pa. His voice quivered with excitement.

"I hope not," Uncle Elbert said, frowning. "You'd break your fool neck, for sure."

Johnny glanced at Pa. His short head sat squarely on broad shoulders. When Pa moved his head forward, the rest of him moved with it.

"Well, I'm gonna do it," Pa insisted. "One day, I'll fly off this here mountain like them red-tailed hawks. Just look at 'em! There ain't nothin' prettier than a red-tail catchin' the breeze for a free ride. Beats coasting down the mountain on a dirt bike any day."

Uncle Elbert frowned at his brother. "Pity you ain't a bird, Earle, but you ain't. I'm afraid you're too keen on a bad idea. And I know you, little brother. You was always sure you could do anything you took a notion to. Them people out there had to learn a lot and then practice. Even the best of 'em take a big chance every time they go up." He shook his head. "Nobody can tell when the air around this rock's gonna change quick. A body could get sucked slam against the side of the mountain."

"I'll learn to do it right," Pa said stubbornly.

"Forget it, Earle. High flying of any kind ain't for a Finlay," Uncle Elbert said in his usual sensible tone. "You ain't forgot you got a family to look after, have you?"

"Hawks got families, too," quipped Ray Arthur, causing Pa to chuckle.

Uncle Elbert glared at Ray Arthur. "Nobody asked you," he clipped without smiling. He turned back to his brother. "As for them hawks, you'd best not mention them favorably to Aunt Lou."

Pa winked sideways at his son. But Johnny knew Uncle Elbert had seen the determined look in his father's eyes. He also remembered how fast a hawk had once swooped down and hoisted away one of Aunt Lou's pullets right under her nose.

"Smart devils," Aunt Lou had snapped. "They just set up there in that tall tree and pick out which one of my chickens to take. They can see 'em five-hundred yards away!"

Johnny hoped Aunt Lou didn't find out about Charley. That morning, he and Pa had slipped a bit of meat from the fridge so the hawk would have a snack when they visited the loft. But Charley needed more food today. Johnny hadn't made it to Aunt Lou's barn to set any traps. And it was clear that he wasn't likely to get anymore of Pa's attention or help today.

An uneasy feeling bit its way through him. When Pa took a notion to do something, he wasn't one to put it aside. He wondered how much a big kite cost. But no matter; whatever the cost, Pa couldn't afford it. Money wasn't something the Finlays had to throw around.

Uncle Elbert, the older brother, had always been the serious one. He'd worked hard and built a successful business. Pa had bounced about the mountain, flirting with disaster by moonshinin' with Corn Kelly all those years before Pa came to the Lord. Since getting saved, he had really tried to be more practical, but his little-boy ways kept splashing up like fish jumped in Way-High Creek. Yet Pa was more fun than Uncle Elbert, who owned the Highway Store where he'd given his brother a steady job.

"Come out of it, Johnny." Ray Arthur snapped his fingers in front of Johnny's nose. "You said you had plans for the rest of the day. What are they?"

"I do," Johnny said. "Can you keep a secret . . . from Aunt Lou, I mean?" He led the way through the woods.

Ray Arthur's merry green eyes twinkled. "You know you can count on me," he promised, "'cept she's apt to be on to whatever it is, already."

Johnny laughed, then told him about Charley, the hut, and his plan for the hawk's meal today.

"Aunt Lou's with the women at my house, so it's a good time," Johnny said.

"This sounds like a job for Midnight the Mighty Mouse Catcher," quipped Ray Arthur in a deep, put-on voice.

Catching mice was one of Midnight's favorite things to do. However, teaching the dog to release his catch on demand had taken lots of patience and time. Johnny was glad he and Ray Arthur hadn't given up on it.

Today in Aunt Lou's barn, they cheered as the big black dog accepted the challenge. He sniffed and scratched in the corn bin till they had five fat mice for the paper bag. Then Johnny twisted its top and tied a string around it.

They found some traps in the barn. With part of a pimento cheese sandwich saved from the church picnic, they baited them. After setting the traps in dark corners, the boys hurried through the woods to the hermit hut.

When Johnny entered the hawk loft, Charley raised his crest as if to greet him. The bird glared hard at Ray Arthur's red hair. Then Charley's attention was totally centered on the meal set before him.

5
Much Ado about Flying

On Tuesday, Johnny woke up to the soft sound of his sister, Louise, strumming on Pa's guitar. A warm, peaceful feeling went over him as he thought: *Summer will soon be here.* He could hardly wait to be free from school again. Then he could fish and swim in Way-High Creek. He'd have time to gather wild herbs for Aunt Lou. Best of all, he might help Hank and Rusty save the trees on the mountaintop.

Johnny had wasted last summer by suspecting the two young motorcyclists were up to no good. How silly he had felt when he learned they were students in the School of Forestry at Jimson College. Johnny hated to see sick trees. It hurt him to watch strong young trees grow up, then die. Now that he had decided to be a conservationist, he looked forward to the return of Hank and Rusty to work on the problem. He just hoped Charley would be on his own by then.

Thus far, the hawk's food had arrived as needed. Sunday afternoon, a big bluejay crashed into the church's glass door. "A gift from above," Sandy called it. Three fat "church mice" completed the bird's meal for Monday.

Johnny hoped he'd be half as blessed in getting today's rations for Charley.

"Johnny Elbert . . . Louise!" It was Ma's "get up or else" call. He yawned and eased out of bed.

At breakfast, Pa was still bragging about his intended flight from Mirror Mountain. He hadn't stopped talking about it since Sunday.

"Earle Finlay," Ma protested, "you ain't got enough life insurance for such craziness." She sighed. "And I reckon there's other reasons we ain't hankerin' for you to get yourself smashed on them rocks at the foot of the mountain."

"Well, for goodness sake, I would hope so," spoke up thirteen-year-old Louise, indignantly. Her slender fingers coaxed long, honey-blonde strands of hair away from her cheeks.

"Aw, I ain't gonna do nothin' stupid," Pa argued. "I'll do it right, Mae Beth, the way I keep bees that make the best sourwood honey on this here mountain." His voice lowered to a mumble about how he once made the best moonshine, too.

It wasn't lost on Ma's ears. "And did the most time

for it, too, don't forget. Your givin' that up was the best thing that ever happened to this family. Now, Big Man, just get on that little dirt bike and ride!" Ma started singing: "Ride, ride to the Highway Store. . ."

Pa crossed his eyes to fix their mother with a devilish grin. Johnny and Louise giggled as Ma, half-smiling, half-frowning, lifted the broom as if to whack him.

Pa ducked and managed to stick out his tongue before making a quick exit. It was hard to stop laughing when Ma threatened anyone with her trusty, yet harmless broom. "Get movin'," she commanded, "or for sure, I'll sweep you all out that there door!"

At school, Scott was waiting beside the green door. He swung a small cooler. As Johnny reached his friend, he could feel Louise's puzzled eyes on them. *Just ignore her*, he told himself.

"I froze the scraps so they'd stay fresh," Scott said.

After the cooler was safe in Johnny's locker, he asked, "What's new?"

"Cecil's Mom and Dad are getting a divorce," Scott said. The serious look in his brown eyes failed to mar Johnny's jovial mood.

"A divorce?" he echoed, then grinned widely. "Anybody'd want to get away from Cecil Harwood."

With his fist, Scott landed a playful jab on Johnny's arm. "Don't be funny," he chided. "Cecil's a pest, for sure, but he is really upset about this."

When they reached the classroom, Johnny stole a glance at Cecil. He looked different, sad and a little lost. For one thing, he didn't have his foot in place to trip someone the first chance he could get. Putting people down was Cecil's specialty, but not today. The green-eyed boy sat quietly at his desk, chin in hands. His face was mapped out with lines of worry. *This ought to be a nice change*, thought Johnny, *Cecil behaving himself*. For some reason, though, he couldn't feel good about it.

"Johnny, you must have had a busy week-end. It's obvious you didn't study," Miss Blair said after he'd stammered through the reading assignment. He blushed and braced himself to ignore the snorts and snickers he'd come to expect from Cecil. None came.

"Cecil needs to get his mind off the trouble at home," Scott said at recess. "Maybe we could help."

Johnny frowned, puzzled. "How can we do that?"

"I was thinking about our club." Sparks of an idea flashed in Scott's eyes. "Cecil and Willis could ride with me and Dad and . . ."

"What'd you say?" Johnny's eyes stretched almost round. "Feelin' sorry's one thing. But you know I don't cotton to bringin' that little twerp into our club. It . . . it'd be too close to thrive." He'd heard Aunt Lou say that when relatives visited too long. With Cecil, he could say it before a visit started.

"But we need help to fix up the hermit hut," argued Scott. "You know it's time to forget some things. It's just right for us to help Cecil through a bad time."

Saying no to Scott was never easy. And maybe he was right, too. Johnny had almost shed his bad feelings over the rotten time Cecil had given him last fall. His problems in coming back to school after missing three years weren't all caused by Cecil. He'd give the boy that. Cecil had not singled Johnny out. The chance to ridicule any classmate when that person was down was something Cecil seldom passed up.

As for Scott, how could he refuse to go along with him? Hadn't he chosen Johnny, a corny-talking mountain boy for a friend? And at a time when everyone else was laughing at him.

"I reckon we could give him a try," Johnny heard himself say, "if his folks let him come. But don't forget how Mrs. Harwood spread the word 'bout Pa servin' time? She might not let him come up on the mountain."

Scott squared his shoulders and shook his head. "No problem. What Cecil wants, he gets! My Mom says it's awful how his parents try to outdo each other buying him presents and never saying no to him."

"Well, maybe *they* jump when he snaps his fingers, but he can't have his way about everything on Mirror Mountain. And that's for sure," vowed Johnny.

"No," Scott agreed. "We'll let any new members know first off. You're president, and I'm vice-president. That way, they'll know who's in charge."

Johnny couldn't imagine Cecil understanding what it meant for anyone to be "in charge." Whatever came of this idea of Scott's, it wasn't likely to be boring.

"Another thing," Scott went on, "we ought to name the club before we invite them. What do you think of calling it the 'Hobo Club'?"

"Naw," Johnny objected. "Hermit Dan wasn't no hobo."

Scott's eyes brightened. "I know! Let's call ourselves 'The Hermiteers.' "

"I like it," Johnny agreed. They slapped hands.

Inviting Cecil and Willis to the mountain was like giving Midnight a piece of steak. The faces of both boys shone like tinfoil all day long. Johnny decided Cecil's slurs about Mirror Mountain must have come from jealousy, after all.

"Will they be hang gliding Saturday?" Cecil wanted to know. He had a thing about flying—always bragging about becoming an aviator when he grew up.

"If the weather's right," Johnny promised. He was surprised to find himself feeling better about the turn of events. Cecil's sadness seemed to be over for the time being.

At the library, Johnny saw the two boys checking out hang gliding books. It made him think of his parents' argument at breakfast. Funny, he thought. Pa wanted to fly. Cecil wanted to fly. Was this going to cause him more trouble? More, maybe, than finding food to keep an injured hawk so it could fly again?

6
Spooked on Top Trail

After school, Johnny got off the bus in front of Aunt Lou's. He hid the cooler of meat scraps behind an azalea bush near the road.

Aunt Lou was in the chicken yard. A thick roll of chicken wire stood by the gate.

"Your Uncle Elbert brought it up today," she said. "Now we just got to get it over the top of the yard."

A long pigtail of silver hair swung like a string of pearls from her calico bonnet. Though Johnny was short for a boy almost twelve, he was still taller than his great aunt. But woe to anyone who was fooled by her size. Aunt Lou was ninety pounds of unbeatable grit.

"It'll take a powerful lot of wire to cover that yard,"

he told her. His eyes went over the area.

"Well, I'm gonna try and do most of it," she declared, hands on hips. "I'm tired of them hawks making off with my chickens."

"We're gonna need posts down the middle to line up with the side ones," speculated Johnny. "Even then, that wire ain't gonna lay tight." Pa had taught him how to cover a chicken yard. "It'll crimp up and sag," he informed her.

"No matter." Aunt Lou fixed her mouth in a stubborn line. "Just so's nothin' can fly in."

"Maybe it ain't hawks that's gettin' them chickens, Aunt Lou. There's foxes and weasels and . . ."

"Don't try to talk me out of it," she snapped. "Them pullets get snatched with no signs a'tall. That's hawks. There's some posts stacked back of the barn. I'll fetch the post hole digger."

Johnny wanted to tell his great aunt what Sandy had said about a hawk's diet: that small rodents made up ninety-nine percent of a red-tail's food. *No,* he decided. *She'd just wonder why I'm taking up for the big birds.* Once she'd made up her mind, Aunt Lou wasn't easily persuaded.

Throughout the afternoon, Johnny dug post holes. The idea had one bright spot: it might put an end to the danger all hawks were in from Aunt Lou's .22 rifle. What saved them now was her failing eyesight. There was a time when the little woman used her rifle as skillfully as a fly swatter.

That afternoon there wasn't time to string the wire.

Johnny hand-shelled several ears of corn for the chickens. A new brood of Rhode Island Red chicks cheeped about the yard. For a moment, he thought about pocketing a couple of the furry little biddies for Charley's supper. A devilish smile sparked his short, wide face. Of course he couldn't do it. Seeing rats die was bad enough. There was a limit to what he could do for Charley's sake.

Louise had asked too many questions about the cooler this afternoon. She wasn't easily put off, either. And if there was anything a sister could be besides nosy, it was a blabbermouth.

He checked the six mouse traps Ray Arthur had helped him set. The four dead mice in them had begun to smell.

"It's a good thing I don't need 'em today," he murmured. He tossed them out of the barn's back window. Two days was too long to wait to empty traps, he decided. He needed the kind that didn't kill the rats. Pa might have an idea about that. Pa could even build one himself if he took a notion to. Then he could set it in the hut. Charley's rations could be delivered to him alive and kicking, the way a hawk preferred them.

The sun was low in the west when Johnny left Aunt Lou's. Midnight wanted to follow, but Aunt Lou called the dog to supper. Midnight knew his duty after sundown: guard his owner's cabin.

As Johnny passed his own house, he dropped the knapsack of books on a big rock near the road. He was glad Ma wasn't on the back porch working on willow baskets. But the way she could lose herself in handicrafts, she might not have noticed the cooler even if she had been there.

It was almost dark when he reached the hawk loft. Charley seemed to expect him. The bird watched closely as the meat scraps were emptied on the board. He didn't seem afraid of Johnny, just glad the food had arrived. Perhaps the bird had a family nearby. If so, he must need to get back to them. When young babies were in the nest, the father and the mother had to take turns gathering food and guarding the nest.

Sandy had refilled the water bucket. Johnny changed the water in the basin, with Charley's sharp eyes missing nothing.

"Now, don't you go frettin' yourself," Johnny said. "You're gonna be back up there with your folks 'fore you know it."

He closed the door to the loft and glanced at the hut on his way out. He shuddered. The small building had a haunted look in the gray dusk. He hurried past and around the rock formation.

A shadowy mist had crept across Top Trail. The gaunt corpses of trees looked like angry creatures that seemed to move in slow motion. He thought of the foggy scenes where nothing looked right in scary TV shows. He whistled a tune—or tried to. The air grew chilly, curling around his ears. Rumors of Hermit Dan's ghost whirled about in his brain.

"I don't believe nary one of 'em!" he told himself.

The toes of his sneakers kicked up leaves as he walked fast.

He clenched his teeth and lifted his taut chin high. Then he shouted: "I'M JOHNNY ELBERT FINLAY, PROTECTOR OF WILD LIFE!" Lowering his voice, he stammered, "N-nothin' on this here mountain scares m-me."

Johnny stopped walking. There was no breeze. Out of the silent shadows, he was sure something had sounded—rustling, or scraping not far behind him. Or was it just the pounding of his heart? His hand tightened on the cooler handle.

When a boy's head sat right on his shoulder, he couldn't turn it quickly without taking the rest of him along. He pivoted. About a hundred yards away, his eyes made out the sinister silhouette of a man against the thin haze that filled the twilight air. . . at least it looked like a man: long hair like wild grape vines stripped of their leaves. Gnarled and straggly, the figure waited, unmoving. A chilling quiet hung over the whole forest. Just then, Johnny would have been glad for any sound at all: the tinny cluck of a chipmunk or a bobwhite's whistle, even the woeful hoot of an owl.

Instead, there was only the heavy silence. Frozen to the spot, Johnny watched the figure begin to float slowly into the woods on the west side of Top Trail. Moving in the opposite direction from Hermit Dan's hut, the apparition disappeared.

Like any boy who is sure he just saw a ghost, Johnny turned and started running. Soon his sneakers slapped across Mirror Rock and pattered, lickety-split, down the road toward his home.

The good smell of country ham greeted him, and he hurried in to supper. It seemed to Johnny that it took half the meal before his heart stopped pounding.

"What's eatin' you?" asked Ma. "You don't look right, and you ain't said one word."

"Nothin'," shrugged Johnny. Luckily Ma was too busy talking about a new dress she wanted to make Louise to pursue her questions any further.

Later, Johnny cornered Pa near the beegums under the big sourwood tree.

"Them traps I set in Aunt Lou's barn ain't workin' out," he said.

"Reckon that figures," Pa said. "You need somethin' that'll catch rats alive and hold 'em." His eyes started the bright smile of an idea that soon spread over his face. "I can get one from the store."

"Will it cost much?"

"Not with my employee's discount," Pa wiggled his pug nose. "I'd make one myself, but time's too scarce."

Johnny heaved a sigh of relief. "You just made my day," he said. "I'm glad you're my pa.

"Pa," Johnny started to say as Pa's strong arm went around his shoulder. Then he stopped. He couldn't tell his father about the ghost just then. Pa wasn't afraid of anything, and Johnny didn't feel at all brave tonight.

7
Pa to the Rescue

After rounding Dead Man's Curve the next afternoon, Sandy stopped the homebound bus abruptly. He handed a litter bag to Johnny and said, "Get that dead rabbit by the road. Just be sure it's freshly killed."

The rabbit's body was still warm. After sliding it into the bag which he twisted at the top, Johnny laid the "road-kill" at his feet in the bus. Then he followed Sandy's glance toward Louise, who sat in the back seat. Her face was a mixture of confusion and disgust.

"What'd you plan on doin' with that?" snapped Louise with disgust. "You gonna bury it, or somethin'?"

Johnny decided not to answer, but he could see that Sandy was having trouble keeping his green eyes serious.

"You know, if you'd left it by the road, a red-tail would've got it," Louise offered. "I bet you got some gruesome plans that has to do with that old cooler you been luggin' around. I'm gonna find out what's in it."

Johnny fixed his sister with a silly face, then turned away from her and grinned. Finding food for Charley might not be easy, but it sure wasn't boring.

Wednesday was the afternoon that Sandy tutored Johnny. But before they got started, they took the rabbit to the hawk loft. Charley was pleased to have a change in his menu. Besides the rabbit, each carried two gallons of water in plastic milk jugs. Sandy had made a rule. No trip was to be made anywhere near the hut without jugs of water.

A short time later, Johnny sat with his books before him on the table in the log church. He told Sandy of his decision to become a protector of wild life.

"A conservationist!" marveled Sandy. "That just might be God's plan for you, Johnny."

"But that long word ain't easy to spit out."

"Get your dictionary," ordered Sandy. Johnny discovered the word had five parts called "syllables." Working with parts, he was soon able to pull the word together. It was like adding to get a total.

"Con-ser-va-tion-ist. Con-ser-va-tion-ist." He repeated it over and over. The word came easier to his lips.

Sandy gave him a small spiral notebook that fit in the pocket of his jeans. "If you want to be a conservationist, you need to learn how to keep records," Sandy said. "I'll help you."

On the blue cover, Johnny printed: "CHARLEY." Then, remembering back to when they had found the hawk, he slowly wrote on the first page:

> *April 12*: Today we found a red-tailed hawk in a ravine. His wing was sprained. Sandy put him in the hawk loft by Hermit Dan's hut. We will feed him till he gets well enough to fly again.

One page was allowed for each "hawk note" to follow. Sandy made him look up and correct all misspelled words.

"Each Wednesday, the log will be your writing assignment," Sandy promised.

In the past, the time for reading and writing usually seemed endless for Johnny, no matter what Sandy did to try and make it interesting. But today was different. Working on Charley's logbook was almost as much fun as arithmetic.

Just before sundown, Johnny met his father at the end of the driveway. On his head Johnny put the second helmet that Pa kept for anyone brave enough to be a passenger on his dirt bike. Together, father and son zipped over the flat surface of Mirror Rock toward Top Trail. They left the bike by the head-high rock that guarded Hermit Dan's path.

When they reached the hut, Pa opened a bag and brought out the new rat trap. It was a square metal box with tiny holes for ventilation. On one side, beneath a wind-up key, a rat-sized hole gaped.

"This here trap's automatic," Pa told him. "You just bait it with somethin' smelly." He struck a match to singe the edges of cheese scraps he'd brought. Lifting the lid, he placed the cheese in position.

"I see," Johnny exclaimed, "when the rat steps on that there trigger, it chucks him to the other side 'fore he gets his cheese—then he can't get back out!" His eyes twinkled. "Old Charley's gonna love gettin' real live food every meal," he predicted. "Thanks, Pa."

Pa beamed with pleasure. "You're mighty welcome, Son," he said softly.

As they rode back toward Mirror Rock, Johnny tried to look on each side of Top Trail. Tiny creatures scuttled away from the bike's path. He giggled. Even a ghost would take off if it heard Pa coming. He didn't feel a bit scared when his father was with him.

The next day Johnny told Scott about the night he had seen something floating across the trail behind. Scott was real excited over the possibility of a "real" ghost haunting Mirror Mountain. "Do you think it stays at the hermit hut?" he asked.

"Only if it's really a ghost," Johnny said. "Ain't no livin' bein' gonna sleep on a mattress full of rats." He scratched his head. "I don't know what it was I saw that night on Top Trail. I ain't scared, or nothin'. But I'll tell you one thing, I ain't goin' up there by myself after sundown no more."

Scott wanted to tell Cecil and Willis about the

ghost. Johnny agreed. He hoped it might scare them from visiting the mountain. That would be just fine with him. But as it turned out, the ghost story only added to their excitement.

After school that day, Johnny found Aunt Lou sewing crinoline cut-outs on quilt squares. She squinted hard through the drugstore spectacles she'd owned as long as he could remember.

"You oughta get your eyes checked for glasses," he told her.

She heaved a weary sigh. "Maybe so. Close work makes me impatient these days."

Johnny wiggled his toes inside his sneakers. "Aunt Lou, I. . .uh, thought I'd go get them birch twigs you been wantin' for tea."

She peered at him and smiled. "Now, that's a real nice thought. I want to finish these squares today. The church women are makin' a wedding-ring quilt for Brenda Larry. That's Tom Larry's girl. She's gettin' married, come June. They live in town, you know."

She moistened the end of a thread, then held her needle to the window light. After making several unsuccessful attempts to thread the needle, she gave it to Johnny. It took him only a second to do it for her.

"I'll feed the chickens 'fore I go," he said.

"Get a snack from the fridge first," the little woman ordered.

In the kitchen, he cut a huge slice of cheese, tucked it in his pocket, and went to feed the chickens.

With Midnight beside him, Johnny stopped at the

end of his own driveway to pick up two jugs of water. He'd left them behind a bayberry bush before school that morning.

When he opened the door of the hermit hut that day, more than one rat could be heard moving in the trap's holding chamber. Now, he only needed to manage to let them out—one at a time—for Charley.

Midnight was ecstatic over the age-old rat smell coming from the trap. Johnny shoved the dog back with his foot. Then he squeezed through the door to the hawk loft, pulling it shut after him.

Charley plummeted to the board at once, his head cocked jauntily to one side. With his curved bill, he tapped the rat trap, peering into the tiny holes on its side. He was one excited hawk.

"Hold it!" Johnny ordered. "You can't handle but one of these critters at a time."

Carefully, Johnny's short, stubby fingers eased up a corner of the lid. A healthy looking rat pushed through the crack. Quickly, Johnny clapped the lid down. Just as quickly, Charley's sharp talons closed on the rodent with a fatal grip. In no time, the hawk's meal of six limp rats was spread pell-mell over the board. Charley, however, kept pecking at the trap. Johnny had to open it to convince him of its emptiness.

Johnny's face twisted in disgust. "I reckon it's all part of bein' a hawk," he concluded. But he couldn't help feeling sorry for the rats. They'd had no chance at all.

A few minutes later, Johnny stood on the ledge overlooking the valley below Mirror Mountain. If he could only shuck the memory of the merciless slaughter he'd just seen. He wished the view of the greening meadow could blot it from his mind. It wasn't easy to accept the overall plan of the wild. For each living creature to exist, others had to die.

"That's how the good Lord planned it," Pa had explained. "It ain't always pretty, but if man messes with that plan, nothin' don't work right anymore. If big animals didn't eat the little 'uns, they'd overrun this whole mountain." And Sandy had agreed with Pa.

Far be it from me to mess up nature's balance, Johnny thought. Sighing, he baited the trap again with the cheese from his pocket. He put it back in the hut. As he left, Johnny crossed his hands over his chest and bowed deeply toward the hawk loft. "From now on, your majesty, Charley Hawk," he announced with aplomb, "you have food on the premises."

Midnight barked approval, then bumped against Johnny on the way to get the twigs for Aunt Lou's sweet birch tea.

That night, Pa brought home some galvanized wire. "Them rabbits," he told Ma and Louise, "has been strippin' your marigold seedlings, in case you ain't noticed. I'm gonna trap 'em for you."

After supper, they turned on the one light bulb in the old woodshed near the bee hives. There, Pa and Johnny worked till bedtime. Not only did they finish a small rabbit trap, they also built a rat-holding cage into which Johnny or Sandy could transfer the daily catch. When the trap door was lifted, only one rat could run out before the operator let it fall again. A daily supply of live rats would now be available for Charley. Sandy wouldn't need to pick up any more road kills. Hopefully, the rabbit trap would offer a change in menu from time to time.

It was good to have a father who understood all about feeding a hawk, thought Johnny.

8
The Air Thickens

"But I thought you had Thursday afternoons off?" Ma's voice was threaded with disappointment.

"Next week, I will," Pa answered. "That's a promise, Mae Beth."

"Your brother ought to stick with what he says." She wore a yellow flowered dress, and her shining brown hair was caught up in a ponytail at the back. It seemed to go with Ma's slender face and high cheekbones.

This morning's breakfast was Johnny's favorite: eggs, chopped onions, and potatoes scrambled together. Something wasn't right, though. He watched Pa studying his coffee. Maybe it was the way that stubby finger of his slid up and down the mug's handle. Then it hit Johnny. His father wasn't telling the truth. Suddenly his food seemed to stick in his mouth.

Pa's plans for the afternoon didn't include work at the store. Nor did they include Ma. Johnny felt sure this was true. A hollow place in his stomach did a big flip-flop. Since Pa had become a Christian, the Finlays had never been happier. Evenings weren't ruined by wondering when his father would get home from making moonshine with Corn Kelly.

Pa didn't drink anymore. He kept reminding his children always to tell the truth. So why didn't he just come out in the open with today's plans? That way Ma could just be mad and get over it. Or would she? Did Pa plan to do something that might deeply hurt her feelings? Was that what had happened with Cecil's parents? The thought made Johnny's stomach churn.

"Please don't let him hurt Ma," Johnny prayed silently. It was what Sandy called a "shooting prayer." He knew God heard it, because his stomach settled right down to enjoying breakfast again.

At school, Cecil's old hostility toward Johnny was no longer showing. If the boy wasn't whispering about ghosts, he was drawing hang gliders on every book cover.

"I found this parachute cloth in the garage," Cecil told the other boys. "I'm gonna build myself a hang glider—or maybe a parachute. My dad was a pilot in the Air Force, you know."

They knew. Cecil had told them so just about every day that year.

Cecil's talk made Johnny uneasy. "We'll go watch

the kites take off if the south wind's a'blowin'," he promised. "But we got work to do at the hut. You ain't gonna have time to build nothin'."

He hoped Cecil would realize his idea to build a glider or parachute would go nowhere. He wished Scott had thought of some other way to help Cecil cheer up, a way that wouldn't involve Johnny.

Problems, problems, problems, he thought. Louise was another one. Too many people were finding out about Charley. He and Louise used to share secrets. He had to admit his big sister had some good, sensible ideas. Of course, he couldn't let her know he paid much attention. But Charley was different. If she found out about the hawk, she'd tell Ma, and Ma would tell Aunt Lou. He definitely didn't want a showdown with his great aunt—not yet, anyhow.

After school, he finished stringing the wire across the chicken yard. Aunt Lou inspected the finished job and gave him a quick hug.

"Your Pa couldn't have done better," she told him. "Now, don't go worryin' your head about helping me Saturday. You got them classmates comin'. A boy needs some time to be with other young'uns."

At supper, Ma was too quiet. Pa had come in acting frisky as a pup—too frisky for someone who was supposed to have worked all day. Then, when supper was over, he dismissed the children and insisted on helping Ma with the dishes.

Johnny knew he shouldn't eavesdrop, but he was bent on hearing what his parents said. Under a kitchen window, he hunkered close to the house.

"How'd you know I wasn't at the store this afternoon?"

"Not from you, for sure!" Ma sounded hurt. "Lizzie West came by on her way home from the store."

Miss Lizzie, who weighed every bit of two hundred pounds or more, had a big mouth, too. She was the one who had started the rumors about Hermit Dan's ghost. She'd seen it herself, she claimed. "That ghost was a'lookin' for them goats, most likely."

"Busy Lizzie!" hooted Pa. "Our house ain't on her way home and you know it!" Irritation mounted in his voice. "Likely as not, you asked . . ."

"You know me better'n that," snapped Ma. "She came right out and told me she asked for you to wait on her. Ray Arthur told her you was gone for the afternoon."

A long, heavy pause followed. Then Pa's voice got natural again. He'd been at the college, he said. Ma came back that it didn't seem likely, seeing how he hadn't even finished high school. Pa said he'd gone for a hang gliding lesson from Matt Bryan. The way Ma exploded then made Johnny see why Pa wouldn't tell her that before. Pa tried to convince her it wasn't all that risky if you learned the right way to pilot a big kite. Then he bragged how he'd soared a hundred feet today.

"You just wait. One day I'm gonna throw myself off Mirror Rock and . . ."

"Hogwash!" Ma interrupted. "Where'd you get one

of them things, anyhow? We sure ain't got money for such foolishness. A car's what we need. I get tired of always havin' to catch a ride to leave this mountain for anything."

That was when Pa told Ma he was going to buy Mr. Lonnie Shook's old four-wheel-drive station wagon. "Furthermore," said Pa, "I was just rentin' the hang glider. And it warn't that much, either."

"Any cost for something like that's a waste," said Ma. "M-my heart's set on Louise and Johnny goin' to college." She was almost sobbing now.

"I got full intentions of that very thing coming to be," said Pa. "But everyone needs to have a little fun sometimes. You don't seem to smile or laugh much anymore."

Then Pa started getting mushy, saying things like how pretty she looked when she smiled.

"That ain't gonna work, Earle Finlay. We ain't sixteen years old no more. We got a family to think of, or did you forget? I'm plumb sick of your notions. Now you get on out of my kitchen this very minute."

Johnny slipped over to the bent willow couch and sat down. Pa didn't even notice him as he shuffled by, mumbling, with his hands in the pockets of his work pants.

Louise came out and sat down beside him. "The air's thicker'n pea soup when Ma overdoes the cornstarch," she commented.

"I feel like the peace in our house is hangin' over the edge of Mirror Rock," Johnny said. "When Ma and

Pa ain't happy, ain't nobody happy." With tightness in his throat, he swallowed hard and thought about Cecil. Had the trouble between the Hardwoods started this way?

"Well, they been mad plenty of times before," Louise reminded him. "Pa ought not to've started hang gliding lessons without talkin' it over with Ma, first, though."

"What difference would it've made?" Johnny said. "She wouldn't have agreed, and he wouldn't've changed."

"Well, it just isn't right for him to decide somethin' like that and go behind her back with it. It was hurtful for her to find out like she did." Louise shrugged. "Don't worry; maybe things'll be okay tomorrow."

Saturday came early, and Johnny woke up all in one piece. Without yawning or lingering, he pulled on his jeans and T-shirt. He almost wished the boys weren't coming today. He'd like to spend the whole day by himself—fishing, maybe. Then, maybe Pa would come home from work and hug his mother, and everything would be all right again.

"Johnny Elbert," yelled Louise from the other side of the thin partition that divided their rooms. "Either let that dog in, or make him stop that loud scratchin'."

He opened the window and Midnight plopped in. The two of them started for the kitchen. As they passed Louise's room, he poked his head in. "All that sleep ain't makin' you pretty," he teased. As he turned, a bedroom slipper hit his head. He tossed it back.

Fully dressed, Louise bounced out and whacked him hard.

Pa had left for work. After breakfast, Johnny packed frozen wieners and a package of buns in his knapsack. The others would bring the rest of the lunch.

Louise dived into house cleaning by sweeping Midnight out of the door.

"I'm obliged to you for takin' charge of cleanin' on Saturdays," Ma told her, "but ain't you startin' kinda early?"

Louise's amber eyes were shining. "I want to finish and practice a solo for tomorrow. Sandy asked me to sing one I made up. I want to do it right." Her broom picked up speed as she whisked it over the floor.

"Why that's wonderful," Ma said with happy surprise.

Johnny started keeping time with a silly jig, swaying and chanting: "Louise, Louise—won't she freeze; Louise, Louise, don't she shake them knees!"

His sister gave him a brisk swat with the broom. "I hope Hermit Dan's ghost spooks you good today!" she shrieked as he darted out to join Midnight.

9
The Hermiteers

The blue four-wheel-drive van arrived about 9:30 in the morning, bearing three excited boys and an apologetic Mr. Jenkins.

"I tried to tell them it was a bit early," he told Ma, "but they were at my house, driving us mad with their impatience."

Scott wore his usual Saturday garb: big T-shirt and now-faded jeans with lots of zippered pockets. A wink told Johnny the cooler he carried had more than his lunch in it. Cecil and Willis wore new jeans and T-shirts. Willis shouldered a knapsack. But Cecil drug out a fat duffel bag.

"What's in there?" asked Johnny.

"It's just lunch and stuff," Cecil quickly said.

Mr. Jenkins left. As the four boys headed up the road toward Mirror Rock, Johnny noticed Louise watching from the steps.

Midnight darted around the boys in a dance of circles. He kept diving into weeds and bushes after chipmunks or rabbits.

Cecil staggered under the weight of his bag. Twice, they stopped for him to rest. "What'd you bring so much stuff for?" said Johnny.

"It's for my hang glider," said Cecil. "I just didn't want to say nothin' about it back there."

After a quick look at the view from Mirror Rock, Johnny urged them on. "We'll come back when the hang gliders get up here," he promised.

Charley's feeding came first. He scanned the newcomers with his piercing eyes, then ignored them.

"He ain't a pet," Johnny told the younger boys who peered through the crack in the door of the loft. "Sandy says we'll start to wean him from the food board soon—maybe today."

"Will he bite?" asked Willis. His dark eyes seemed to fill the whole circle of his thick glasses.

"Well, he *is* a meat eater," Johnny said with a spark of mischief.

From that moment on, respect for Charley was the order of the day for Cecil and Willis. As Johnny and Scott poured a jug of water into the basin, Charley looked again at the new boys, this time with suspicion. He raised his crest. When his big feathers flared, Cecil and Willis ducked out of the door.

"Sandy says people have to get a license to train hawks in this state," Johnny told Scott.

"I know. I looked it up in the library. Men teach 'em to hunt like dogs."

"I ain't got much heart for killin' critters," admitted Johnny. "Wild things oughta be left alone. They got enough natural enemies."

"I think so, too. The book says the way a person trains a hawk is to get it to depend on him for food."

"Well, I'd just as soon Charley be free to hunt his own food."

A loud shriek from just outside the door startled them. Cecil and Willis were pointing toward the hut, their faces stretched with terror.

"Somethin's in there!" Cecil squealed. "We heard it move," added Willis, straightening his glasses.

"The ghost! The ghost!" Scott whispered loudly. His eyes sparkled with excitement.

Johnny crept to the dusty window. He cleared a circle on the glass with his balled-up fist. Then he reared back his short head and laughed.

"What's so funny?" Cecil demanded, pouting.

"What I plumb forgot myself," Johnny managed to say. He swung open the screen and the regular doors and entered. Soon he emerged, dragging the rat cage Pa had helped him build. Squiggling rats fell over each other, bumping desperately against the wire. After Johnny explained this was Charley's Sunday dinner, the boys settled down for Hermiteer business.

Scott announced that only the offices of Secretary

and Treasurer needed to be filled.

That's not a democratic election," Cecil protested.

"It's fair," Johnny retorted, thinking what a nervy little jerk Cecil was. "We started this here club. We didn't have to ask you in at all."

Scott, as usual, said it in a nicer way. "We'll have another election next year. Then you might get to be president or vice-president." His brown eyes were calm as he met the stubborn glances of the younger boys. "This is how we start," he told them firmly.

Willis said he'd be pleased to be secretary. Cecil said he guessed he'd take care of the money when dues were paid.

"Dues can wait," Johnny said. "Right now, we got to clean up this here hut."

Willis helped Scott and Johnny. Out onto the ledge went the mattress, boxes, and everything resembling trash. Thick dust covered flat pieces of rock Dan had laid patio-style for a floor. Johnny sent the two younger boys to break dogwood branches for a broom. Willis readily agreed, but Cecil grumbled, "You should have told us ahead of time if you expected us to do manual labor," as they headed off into the brush.

"Guess who's breakin' them branches," Johnny chuckled as he and Scott got a fire started to burn the trash.

"Well, it sure ain't Cecil; I can tell ya that," said Scott. "But never mind. Willis can handle it."

The last thing added to the fire was the old mattress. Several smoke-dazed mice scampered out. They raced into the bushes and crevices in the rocks.

While Scott watched the fire, Johnny made a final check in the hut. Through the propped open door and clean window, bright sunlight filled the room. It lit his way to something he hadn't seen before. Something dark struck out from behind one of the shelf-like rocks near the top of the back wall. With a stick, Johnny dislodged what turned out to be a gray, metal box a little larger than a cigar box. He dusted off cobwebs that clung to it and hurried outside.

"Open it, open it!" Scott cried when he saw the box. "Maybe it's Hermit Dan's treasure."

The box wasn't locked. Johnny's fingers trembled as he lifted the lid. Inside was the hermit's Bible that Aunt Lou had hoped to find. A marker stuck out of it. Opening its well-worn cover, Johnny carefully flipped through the thin pages. Hoping to find Dan's full name, the boy's heads went together.

The page marker, an almost paper-thin piece of wood shaped like a bird, was placed at Isaiah 40. The thirty-first verse was underlined in pencil. Beside it, someone had printed some words in the margin. Scott read aloud: "Like my hawk, Enoch, I need wings to get above earthly things that harm the spirit."

Neither boy spoke as Johnny thumbed through the rest of the pages. Then he closed the book and returned it to the box.

"I guess that's all Hermit Dan wanted us to know about him," Scott said.

"Looks that way," agreed Johnny. He took his food

bag out of his knapsack and slipped the box into its place. "Aunt Lou and Sandy'll want this treasure," he decided.

A minute or two later, the other boys came back, trailed by Midnight. Johnny showed Willis how to tie the branches into a broom. The boys were proud of how neat the hut looked after they'd swept it out.

Cecil chose to poke sticks into the fire. It was now mostly coals. After tiring of that, he unfolded the silky white cloth he'd brought.

"I hope you ain't plannin' to fly with somethin' you make from that," Johnny told him. "No homemade glider or parachute'll be safe to take you off more'n a two foot rock. You'd best not waste your time on somethin' dangerous."

Cecil glared at Johnny. "I will if I want to."

Johnny could feel himself getting angry. "Listen here, you . . ."

"Hey! Let's eat!" Scott shouted quickly. The tense moment was over. Johnny got the wieners and buns, and the others brought out mustard, relish, paper spoons and plates. Cecil had a carton of canned soft drinks for all. He'd put them in his bag frozen, so they were still cool.

"Where'd you get the name, 'Hermiteers'?" asked Willis.

"Hermit Dan lived here," Johnny reminded him.

"Hermits are just tramps . . . like Old Horace," Cecil put in. "He eats out of garbage cans."

"It's not the same," Scott said. "A hermit lives in a

house by himself. Horace Tweed is a bum. Where he happens to be at dark is where he sleeps."

"You can smell him a block away." Cecil wrinkled up his nose. "Nobody'd let him in a house, for sure."

"And he wears three sets of clothes," added Willis, "with paper stuffed in-between." He tossed a scrap of hot dog bun to Midnight, who had been on hand throughout the meal to receive such morsels.

"If he's got no home, that don't sound too crazy," Johnny remarked. He scooped up some sand and dumped it on the coals.

Cecil's eyes widened. "Not crazy? A guy that sleeps in boxes and eats garbage? Man, you don't get much crazier than that!"

"I still hate to see Mr. Kelly running him away from behind his store," Scott said. "Horace likes to sleep in the big, empty boxes back there."

Cecil sighed heavily. "At least he doesn't have to wonder which folks he'll be living w-with." His voice broke.

A dark silence followed. Cecil stared off the ledge. Johnny was glad for the distant roar of vehicles.

"Last one to Mirror Rock's a rotten potato!" he yelled.

This time Matt Bryan wasn't with the group that launched their colorful kites from the rock. The boys lingered to watch until the distant soarers could hardly be seen in the distant blue.

All the way back to the hut, Cecil talked nonstop. He rehashed his ideas for making a hang glider:

how he'd cut and attach the cloth to cords; the harness and control bar he would make.

Johnny walked slowly behind the others. He was tired of Cecil's babbling and wanted to tell him to shut up. But he realized that it was best for him to keep his distance right now.

The others rounded a curve and were out of sight. Midnight suddenly bounced across the trail in front of him. Johnny watched as the dog ignored him and plunged into a clump of rhododendrons. He stopped. Something had moved where Midnight was. Or someone. Johnny's eye caught a glimpse of green that was a darker shade than any green thing in the woods. He waited. Why didn't Midnight growl, bark, or come back? Then he whistled, but the dog didn't respond. He whistled again, louder. Midnight eased from the bushes, paused and looked back. A third whistle brought him sprinting back to Johnny. Patting the dog's head, he kept his eye on the rhododendrons. The dark green something didn't move again.

"Hey, Johnny," Scott called from ahead of him. "What's holding you up, man?"

Johnny shrugged. "I'm coming!" he yelled in a loud voice, and moved on.

Sandy was waiting for them at the hut. "You did a great job of cleaning up," he told them.

"Did you check on Charley?" Johnny asked.

"I did, and that wing looks great. I think it's time to cut back his rations."

They chose the second ledge as the best place to

leash Charley outside. For a perch, a small scrub oak was trimmed.

Then Sandy went into the loft and carefully tied short leather straps around Charley's legs. "These are called 'jesses,'" he explained. He cautiously brought Charley out and attached a leash to one of the jesses and then to the perch. The feeding board was moved near the steps where the bird could reach it.

"We'll give him his rations as usual for a few days," Sandy said. "He'll get a sense of freedom, but still be on the leash till we're sure he's ready to fend for himself again."

Charley was excited to be outside. On his new perch, he spread his wings. The injured one was just a little lower than the other.

As the other boys watched Charley enjoy the view of the meadow, Johnny got the tin box from his knapsack. He put it in Sandy's hands. "Something I found," he said softly. "You and Aunt Lou's the ones to have it." He glanced over his shoulder at Cecil and Willis. They were busy packing Cecil's hang glider material in his duffel bag. "Wait till you get back to the church to open it," he whispered.

The boys decided they had had a full day. Cecil stored his duffel bag in the hut "till next time," and the boys followed Sandy to the church for a ride home.

When Johnny and Midnight got home, Aunt Lou and Ma were piecing quilt squares together on the back porch. Louise sat on the bent willow couch, strumming the guitar. She had stretched her big dark green T-shirt until it hung nearly to the knees of her faded jeans. The afternoon sun picked up the golden lights in her long hair. Midnight was stretched out at her feet.

In the kitchen, Johnny found and punched a hole in the center of a cold biscuit. He filled it with Pa's sourwood honey and nibbled it as he went out and sat down near Louise.

His sister didn't have a welcoming look, but something had drawn him there. It took him a minute or two to realize it was the dark green shirt. *Darker than the forest leaves,* he thought.

"So it was *you* I saw up on the mountain—a'hidin' in the bushes like a genuine snoop!" he accused. But he had to hear it from her.

She stopped strumming. "Do you think you and your friends have exclusive rights to Top Trail? Or to Hermit Dan's hut where you're feeding a chicken hawk."

Johnny choked on the last bite of honey biscuit. "Hawk?" he asked dumbly.

"Don't act stupid. I saw it while you was up at Mirror Rock. You're dead meat if Aunt Lou finds out."

"She won't—less'n some nosy sister blabs."

"Maybe that's what I ought to do," she clipped with a toss of her chin. "Sandy's in on it, too," she went on. "That's what you two been whisperin' about. Imagine—a preacher pickin' up dead animals on the road!" she shuddered.

A half-informed Louise was dangerous. There was

nothing left to do but tell her the whole story. His dream of being a conservationist was part of it.

As Johnny hoped, Louise relented after learning they planned to return Charley to the wild. She had only resented being shut out.

"You know I can keep a secret when there's need to," she reminded him. "When are you gonna learn to trust my judgment?" She let her hand come down on the guitar strings with a loud *twang*. "And my judgment is, if you're gonna be a conservationist, you got to start talking better grammar. 'Ain't' won't cut it with the educated people you'll have to work with."

"I know," he agreed. "Sandy's helping me. I'm really tryin' to talk better." At least . . . as of that moment, he'd decided he was.

"Good!" she concluded. "Now get lost and let me practice my solo in peace."

10
Too Many Secrets

The congregation of the Church on the Mountain had arranged their chairs in a semi-circle on the gently sloping lawn behind the cabin used as their church meeting house. In front of the people, the deck was just wide enough for Sandy's podium and the choir.

Pa, Uncle Elbert, Louise and her cousin, Cindy Finlay, sang in the choir. Others in the choir were Lonnie and Sara Belle Shook, Mrs. Ethel Carver, and Tom Larry. Of course, Sandy had brought Miss Blair (Johnny's school teacher) who taught the older children's Sunday school class. She also sang in the choir.

Mrs. Ethel Carver, widowed for five years, was pouting after agreeing to shorten her solo, "Farther Along," to one verse and chorus. Johnny was glad Pa'd suggested that. He preferred more of Pa's lively, foot-stomping gospel hymns.

Louise's solo came just before the sermon. Pa checked the tuning of the guitar and passed it over to her.

Johnny couldn't help feeling a bit proud. His sister had sewed her own yellow dress. It brought out the gold in her hair that fell in a loose cloud over her slim shoulders. The look on her face was like Ma's when she wasn't in a hurry.

"God's been tellin' me some things about livin'," said Louise, softly strumming the guitar. "When I watch hang gliders taking people like birds off this mountain, I sometimes wish I can fly away, too, like a butterfly. But the Lord says for me to be still and work hard. Now, that don't . . . doesn't mean my heart has to flatten out. Listen up." She strummed a pretty chord and sang:

People don't have wings
Like birds and pretty angels do,
But my Jesus brings me
A song I can sing, so
He's taught me a way to fly, too.

Johnny closed his eyes and imagined a red-tailed hawk soaring free over the meadows of his mind. Gracefully, its broad wings floated up and down on sun-warmed air.

The second verse talked about how skies were

sometimes grey, but the sun always came out to warm up the air, and make it right for a Christian to fly again. Then, the chorus:

> In my heart I have wings—
> Wings to soar where He sends me;
> My spirit goes higher than I'll ever fly,
> For His love, joy, and peace are within me.
> Wings! In my heart I have wings . . .

Louise's last note faded gently like the echo of a bell.

For a moment, the only sound above the soft swooshing of the nearby creek was some whispered "Amens." Then, everyone stood and clapped. Johnny did, too. For a moment or two, he put aside thinking of Louise as his bossy, big sister.

When everything settled down, Sandy read his text. Isaiah 40:31:

> But they that wait upon the Lord shall renew their strength; they shall mount up with wings like eagles; they shall run, and not be weary; and they shall walk, and not faint.

Sandy McRee preached a good sermon. Even Ray Arthur sat still and listened.

After the picnic, Johnny and Ray Arthur changed clothes and headed for Aunt Lou's to let Midnight out of the barn.

"Aunt Lou's been a'wonderin' if the mushrooms in

the old apple orchard are ready to pick," Johnny said as they walked along.

"You mean 'merkels'," stated Ray Arthur. "Nothin' tastes better'n her merkel pies."

Johnny didn't agree. "I'd rather have apple." It was the time of year when growing boys feel most at home. Like the new life surrounding them, they spread their strong, young arms to catch sun-filled air.

The apples for Aunt Lou's pies came from three big trees. The rest of the orchard was older. It was divided by a little brook that went on to cross a rock plateau. Finally, it became a tiny waterfall that trickled down the mountainside.

"Want to play cowboys and Indians?" Ray Arthur asked. The boys had done just that many times on the plateau.

Johnny didn't answer. His eyes had followed Midnight's swift move forward to the remains of a small fire.

Then Ray Arthur noticed. "Hey! Somebody's been poachin' on our turf!" he cried.

Two half-burned logs lay in ashes of a fire that had been recently smothered. Chicken bones were strewn about, the grease still shiny on them. Midnight gathered them up with gusto.

"Whoever it was ain't been gone very long from here," Johnny observed. "Looks like we found what's been happenin' to Aunt Lou's chickens."

"I thought Midnight was a watchdog."

"Hmmph—I'm startin' to doubt how good he is, too.

At least Midnight ain't eatin' raw chickens. It was no chicken hawk that cooked these bones either. And it ain't. . . I mean *isn't* a ghost, 'cause ghosts don't cook and eat," said Johnny, suddenly remembering his promise to himself to stop saying "ain't."

"Well, it *is* a two-legged thief," concluded Ray Arthur. A further search failed to turn up a culprit or any clue to the whereabouts of one.

Finally, the boys returned to the old orchard to gather the merkels they had spotted earlier.

Aunt Lou was happy to see how well her great nephews had selected the mushrooms with pits instead of folds.

"It is definitely not a hawk that's stealin' your chickens," Johnny said after they'd told her what they found on the plateau.

"Now, Johnny Elbert Finlay, you ain't as sure as you're lettin' on you are!" she came back.

"Well, maybe I'd better sleep over here a few nights," offered Johnny. "If somebody's comin' in your yard . . ."

"How do you know it warn't just some of them campers that like to roam this here mountain? They probably brought their own chicken—cut, dressed, and floured for frying." Her face was fixed in a stubborn mold. "Don't tell me them sorry hawks ain't still figurin' out how to pluck my chickens!"

"I don't see how they can get through that wire," Johnny argued. "And the chickens are still disappearin'."

"Anyway," put in Ray Arthur, "you ought not to be staying by yourself, Aunt Lou."

It was the worst thing Aunt Lou could have heard, and the last thing that would convince her, thought Johnny.

"Nothing's gonna hurt me," she snapped, "and I just better not hear tell of you blabbin' to your folks what you saw—neither one of you!"

"We could think up excuses for me stayin' a night or two," Johnny insisted.

"Save your brainpower!" Her clenched fists were on her hips. "A boy belongs with his ma and pa; not interferin' with an old woman's rest. Me and Midnight'll do just fine."

From way back, they knew it was useless to argue with Aunt Lou. While she washed mushrooms, the boys quietly checked door and window latches.

Later, they went up the mountain to the loft and fed Charley.

That night as he tried to fall asleep, Johnny worried that he should at least tell Pa what they had found. His father seemed so far away, though. Today, he'd noticed how short Uncle Elbert seemed to be toward Pa. Johnny hoped his uncle wouldn't lose patience with his father and fire him. Things were bad enough. Pa getting fired could be the last straw with Ma.

Maybe it wasn't good for people to ever keep things from loved ones. As Louise said, Ma shouldn't have had to find out about Pa's hang gliding lessons the way she did. Of course, Johnny admitted to himself, *he* still wasn't ready to tell Aunt Lou about Charley.

He'd tell her when the bird was returned to the wild.

No one would be hurt by that. But now Aunt Lou was making him keep something from Pa and Uncle Elbert. This was different, for she might be in danger.

We Finlays are a stubborn bunch, thought Johnny. *We don't trust each other a bit if we think telling something might put a stop to our doin' what we want.*

Last week Aunt Lou had gone to an eye doctor for new glasses. When the glasses came, her perfect aim with the .22 could return, and Charley. . .

"Lord," prayed Johnny, "I promise I'll tell her about Charley soon's he's free. You know we can't trust Aunt Lou to understand about hawks. Please just keep her safe from whoever's gettin' her chickens."

11
Runaways

Another Friday had arrived. Johnny sat at his desk after first recess. He took Charley's log book from his pocket and looked over the entries he had made to date.

April 30: We're still feeding Charley. He flies from his perch to the feeding board. I think he could fly anywhere if he wasn't tied down. Sandy says to give the wing a few more days to heal.

May 10: Last night, Scott and I camped out again. Sandy woke us early this morning. It was still dark. We went to the hut. Sandy unfastened Charley's leash, but Charley did not wake up. We put some meat scraps on the board. Then we waited in front of the hut till the sun rose. Charley woke up and jumped to his food. After he ate, he flapped his wings like always. All at once the breeze took him up. He flew over the meadow to some tall trees.

May 17: We're still going up to feed Charley, but he sits in the treetops now. If he flies down to meet us, he gets live rats. If not, we take it to mean he's not hungry. I go up to check every other day. Sandy says its a good sign that he's catching his own food again.

Scott and Cecil and Willis came up on the mountain again today. But Cecil doesn't seem to take much interest in Charley. He wasted most of the day putting what he called "finishing touches" on his homemade hang glider. I have to admit it resembles the big kites. It has cords and a broomstick control bar, but I doubt that it would lift anyone off the ground.

"Where is Cecil?" It was Miss Blair's voice that brought his attention back to the classroom. Her blue eyes were wide with concern.

"Willis is gone, too," Betty Lou Haskell volunteered.

Johnny glanced at the two empty desks, then met Scott's worried glance. All week long, Cecil had walked about with a cloud of gloom hovering over him. Now the little guy was gone. In his confusion and unhappiness, there was no telling what crazy things he might do.

"His parents are having a really ugly fight in court,"

Scott had told him. "Maybe he needs to talk about it."

Cecil *did* talk to the Hermiteers. He seemed to feel more secure with them, as though he could trust them. "I don't know who I'm going to be living with," he told them. "Dad's saying Mom's not fit to raise me. Mom's so mad with him, she wants to stop him from seeing me at all." The boy's eyes were red from crying. The only time he seemed at peace was when he was drawing or reading about hang gliders. By now, he must have stored up a lot of information in his head.

Cecil had run away. Of that, Johnny was certain. In a way he was glad Willis had gone with him. Willis was a good guy in spite of his bookish ways. He might be able to talk Cecil out of doing anything too stupid. But it wouldn't be easy if Cecil had a mind to do something. He was a stubborn one.

The parents of the boys were notified, and an all-out search began. Johnny figured that Cecil and Willis must have left at the beginning of recess. Johnny couldn't remember seeing either of them on the playground.

Their disappearance was the topic of discussion as the yellow station wagon climbed the mountain.

"I can see why Cecil might want to run away," Scott said, "but how could Willis let himself be talked into going along?"

"Where would they go?" Louise wondered.

"The report is," said Sandy, "that two boys answering their description were seen boarding the bus to Asheville."

"That figures," Scott agreed. "Cecil's aunt and uncle live there. I'll bet they phoned for them to meet the bus," he concluded with a look of satisfaction.

"Maybe that's where they wanted people to think they were going," said Johnny. But he wasn't so sure, himself. He knew the bus in question. Many times he'd met it at the foot of the mountain with Aunt Lou's wild herbs. That was how she shipped them to the pharmaceutical company. The bus would be pulling into the Asheville station right about now, and if the boys were on it, they would be found.

A county dump truck met them on its way down the mountain. The trucks still hauled dirt to fill in the road where last winter's rain and snow had washed it away.

Johnny turned to Scott. "What if they ain't . . . aren't on that bus when it gets to Asheville?" he asked in a low voice.

"Where else would they get off?"

"Anywhere," Johnny mumbled. "Like a store or filling station; in front of somebody's house or . . ." his eyes narrowed . . . "at the foot of Mirror Mountain."

Scott's mouth flew open. "Then . . . naw! No way would Cecil walk ten miles uphill."

"He might figure out some other way," Johnny whispered. Sandy brought the bus to a stop in front of Aunt Lou's cabin.

"Mumbling is not a civilized thing to do," Louise informed the boys as they bounded from the bus.

Aunt Lou waved from the front porch as Sandy

drove on. She seemed surprised to see Johnny and Scott. "I thought I saw you two riding on a truck full of dirt awhile back," she said.

After casting knowing glances at each other, the boys looked at her with blank faces. "You got your new glasses yet?" Johnny asked his great aunt.

"They're inside in their case," she said pertly. "I can see you two just fine without 'em."

After putting away some of Aunt Lou's yummy stickies and a glass of milk, the boys went to fetch Bossy from the pasture. They detoured by the apple orchard on the rock plateau. But they found nothing there to suggest that the earlier visitor had been back.

"Let's hope he's gone for good," Johnny said.

After they had tossed fresh hay into the spotted cow's stall and fed the chickens, Aunt Lou loaded the boys down with more than enough food for a night and a day. Into Scott's cooler went fried chicken, sausage biscuits, more delicious stickies, a good supply of pimento cheese, and peanut butter and jelly sandwiches.

At his house, Johnny picked up two extra old blankets. Ma asked why Johnny had never thought he needed more covers for a sleep out before. He told her they'd managed, but you never could tell when a night might cool off fast.

They crossed the log over Way-High Creek, then started setting up their camp for the night.

"Do you think it was Cecil and Willis who Aunt Lou saw on the dump truck?" Scott asked.

Johnny nodded. "I think we're lucky Aunt Lou gave us so much more food this time."

"Shouldn't we go see if they're at the hut?"

"Not till we finish up here. It's more peaceful where Cecil isn't," Johnny said, proud that he hadn't said ain't that time.

Scott grinned. "I knew you wouldn't let anybody go wanting," he said, nodding at the two extra blankets.

Johnny raised his chin. "Don't count too strong on it. I'm just a bit kind when dumb creatures need help."

"They're probably hungry."

"That'll keep. Soon as we get things set up here, we'll take the blankets and see how they're fixed."

The sun was low in the west when they reached the hut. As they had expected, the boys were there.

"I'm never going home," declared Cecil.

Willis pushed his glasses up on his nose. His magnified eyes peered pleadingly at Johnny and Scott.

"What's your plans?" asked Johnny as he and Scott dropped the blankets on the ground.

"To stay here like Hermit Dan forever and ever," piped up Cecil. "That way, I won't have nobody tellin' me what to do!"

Poor Cecil. He didn't use his head at all, thought Johnny, or at least, not the practical part of it.

"How will you feed yourself?" Scott asked.

"I don't know. I'll find a way. Hermit Dan did."

"Cecil, you don't even feed your own dog," Willis put in.

"I can just see Cecil skinning and cooking birds,"

laughed Scott, "and eatin' berries and roots."

"Not to mention milking goats," teased Johnny.

Then Scott got serious. "Have you thought of how worried your parents must be?"

Cecil's bottom lip was poked out far enough to give a crippled cicada bug a ride. "I don't care!" he snorted.

"I do," Willis objected. "I think we ought to go back."

Cecil folded his arms and shook his head. "You planning to sleep here with Hermit Dan's ghost tonight?" Scott asked, raising his dark eyebrows.

"I'm not scared," Cecil declared stubbornly.

"Well, I-I'll stay if you and Johnny do," Willis offered, "unless we can get home tonight."

"We can't sleep here," Johnny said. "Sandy looks for us to be down by the creek. That's the only way our folks'll let us sleep out—with Sandy checkin' on us."

"Sandy would take you home now if he knew you were here," Scott told them.

"No!" Cecil declared. "We'll stay here, but I'm hungry." His look told them he expected them to do something about that little problem.

Johnny made a pie face. "You mean you didn't bring food? Did you think there was a supermarket way up here?"

"The bus tickets took all our allowances," Willis explained. "We paid to go to Asheville." He turned to Cecil. "And that's what we should have done. I told you not to pull that cord to get off!"

Cecil shrugged, but said nothing.

"It wasn't smart," Johnny said, "but what's done's

done. C'mon, Scott. Let's go."

"And leave them all night with no food?"

Johnny patted his sneakered toe on the hard ground, watching the horror-stricken faces of the younger boys. "All right," he agreed after a few seconds. "But wait till dark to come to our camp. And keep out of sight. You can sleep near us, so bring them blankets. If nobody gets too greedy, I reckon we got enough food."

Scott drew his flashlight from his pocket and handed it to Willis. A look of relief went over the boy's round face. Cecil sighed, but said nothing.

"But that's just for tonight," warned Johnny. "First light, we go to Sandy McRee so he can take you home. No ifs, ands or buts."

"I knew you wouldn't leave them up there all alone," Scott said as they got their campfire going a little later.

When Sandy came by to check on them, he said he had to work on a term paper, so he only stayed a few minutes. Johnny hoped he wouldn't regret putting off telling Sandy about the boys. But it seemed right to save him the night trip down the mountain. After all, what could go wrong overnight?

Fireflies had scarcely started flashing their little lights in the woods when Cecil and Willis came tearing from the laurel grove above the creek, blankets clutched under their arms. Their faces were a blend of terror and excitement. It was a wonder they didn't fall off the crossing log into the creek.

"We saw it!" Cecil shrieked, shuddering. "We saw

Hermit Dan's ghost up on Top Trail!"

"I don't believe in ghosts, but I-I saw something, too," echoed Willis.

In tremulous loud whispers, the two boys described the same shadowy figure Johnny had seen on the trail that other night. Now Johnny was sure he hadn't imagined it.

If the boys had been afraid, it didn't seem to interfere with their appetites. Of all the food Aunt Lou had provided, there was barely enough left for breakfast.

Behind some myrtle bushes, Cecil and Willis seemed glad to roll up in their blankets. Thoroughly exhausted from everything that had happened, they fell asleep right away.

Later, from his sleeping bag, Johnny looked at the stars through the pines. *Why couldn't Cecil's parents just agree to let him live one place or the other*? he sighed.

Cecil's parents weren't poor. The boy was spoiled rotten from getting his way about everything. Having enough money didn't seem to make people happy. Johnny was glad Ma and Pa were still together. He was sure they loved each other, even if they kept a quarrel going too long to suit him. A scared little feeling touched him. "Please don't let them stay mad," he prayed. Then drowsiness overcame him.

12
Cecil's Great Flight

Johnny dreamed Ma and Pa weren't speaking to each other. Messages between them had to be delivered by the children. Then the house started shaking.

"Tell your ma we're havin' an earthquake, Johnny Elbert," said Pa.

"Louise, you tell that man I hope it shakes the whole mountain down till he ain't got nothin' to jump off of."

"But, Ma," Louise objected, "we'd all be killed!"

Johnny could feel the quake. He wished it would stop.

"Wake up!" Scott's voice boomed in his ear as he jiggled Johnny's shoulders.

Johnny opened one eye, then shut it against the blinding sunlight. "It can't be day already," he moaned.

"It's late," Scott said. "We slept too long. Cecil and Willis are gone."

"Cecil?" Johnny sat up and rubbed his eyes. "Willis? I thought they'd at least wait to eat somethin'."

"Oh, they got their share." Scott plopped down on his sleeping bag and munched on a peanut butter and jelly sandwich. No one who didn't know better would have taken him for the neat, well-groomed son of a mill owner. His clothes had a wrinkled, slept-in look. Chunks of dark brown hair stood up in untidy fashion above his relaxed, jelly-smudged face. A little smile slowly crept over Johnny's sleepy face as he took in Scott's air of sloppy contentment.

"I didn't think they'd go back to the hut so soon after the scare they had last night." Scott said.

Johnny sighed. "I reckon they didn't figure a ghost'd come out in daylight." He pulled on his sneakers and dashed melted ice water from the cooler on his face. "I'm gettin' Sandy now," he decided, as he lifted the sandwich bag Scott had removed from the cooler. Only one peanut butter-jelly was left. He stuffed it in his mouth and stumbled up the piney slope to the church.

Sandy was already working on his sermon. The news about Cecil and Willis didn't seem to surprise him. "I had a feeling they might come up here," he said. "You should have told me last night."

"I know," agreed Johnny, wishing he had.

"Well, let's get to the hut now." Sandy was up and on his way out of the door. "We've got to get those boys back to their parents right away," he said.

Scott had gone on ahead. As Sandy and Johnny reached the path to the hut, they heard Scott's voice yelling, "No, Cecil—don't do it!"

Then Willis' anxious squeal: "Please, Cecil. It won't work! Stop, pleeease!"

"Oh, no," Johnny moaned knowingly as they quickened their pace around the tall boulders.

Cecil's hands were on the broomstick control bar, with his big white kite billowing above in the breeze. He looked like an overgrown cabbage butterfly. But unfortunately, he was no butterfly, just Cecil Harwood at his obstinate worst.

Before another "stop" was uttered, he took a running start and pushed off the ledge. The leap moved him forward about five feet. Then he took a downward dive and sunk feet-first in the middle of the big patch of briars. The remains of the homemade glider spread like a puffy white blanket over the thorny thicket. When Cecil's small carrot-topped head appeared, his green eyes were stretched wide with terror. And he let out a shrill, blood-curdling wail. Mass paralysis seemed to set in on the group gathered on the ledge.

Scott was first to recover. "Just like B'rer Rabbit!" he shouted. Hysterical laughter spread over the group.

Except for Sandy. "Stay where you are, Cecil," he called in a calm voice. "I'm coming to get you out of there."

Sandy started down the rock steps to the second ledge. Charley's feeding board was halfway between him and Cecil. Above them, the boys had stifled their laughter. For Cecil wasn't in a very comfortable place, and was plainly terrified.

Just as he was beginning to feel relieved, Johnny's ear caught another sound. It was more chilling than Cecil's scream had been. The first time he had heard a rattlesnake shake its tail, he'd been with Pa. "Don't move," Pa had warned. The two had escaped its deadly fangs. Now he could see the frightened reptile, its head raised from a coiled position. It was beside the feeding board, blocking Sandy's way to Cecil.

"Don't say nothin'," he warned Scott and Willis, as he pointed to the snake.

Sandy had seen it in time to stop still on the bottom step. But Cecil was taking time out from screaming just long enough to catch his breath, and the reptile had directed its fangs toward the briar patch. Sandy could only motion to Cecil, who wasn't getting the message.

"Cecil," Johnny bellowed. "It's a rattlesnake lookin' at you. Shut up and don't move a muscle!" He didn't know he could yell so loud, and hoped the noise didn't cause the snake to turn on Sandy, who was nearest to its poisonous fangs. He breathed deeply when he saw Cecil's scratched, red face pale as he realized that the rattlesnake was interested in him.

Johnny felt pulled apart. For just a second he scolded himself for not telling Sandy last night. If he had, this wouldn't be happening. Now there wasn't time to run for help. "Please send a miracle," he prayed.

Scott and Willis were like statues, their faces frozen with fear. Any second, the snake could strike. It wasn't a big one, but that didn't make it harmless. The noisy rattlers were proof of that.

Into the perilous moment, a swift shadow jetted from above and landed several feet away from the snake, facing it.

"Charley," Johnny whispered loudly. The hawk had not met him at the board for several days.

Charley flared his body plumage, raising his crest, and the snake was no longer interested in Cecil. The big bird's wings were spread to full beauty as he danced a jig of graceful swiftness. The snake struck at him, but Charley evaded the reptile's lunge. Feinting and bobbing like a prize fighter in a championship ring, the red-tail hopped to the right, circling the coiled serpent. The rattler adjusted so it faced Charley and struck again. The hawk swung its heavy wings forward as its body sprang back. Johnny thought the snake's fangs had caught the great bird's left wing, but instead the reptile's body slapped harmlessly on the rocky ground.

Then, with incredible agility, Charley suddenly pounced back upon the snake and closed strong talons around its neck. Instantly, the deadly creature took on the appearance of a limp rope as its back was broken in the bird's powerful grip. Then the big bird hoisted it up and flew away.

Across the sunlit meadow, all eyes followed the hawk's flight to the top of one of the tallest pines. His red tail glowed in the warmth of the warm morning sunshine.

"Some baby hawks are gonna be happy with their breakfast this mornin'," Scott speculated. "That was truly awesome!"

"Thanks," Johnny said. It was to Charley, but more to God for the miracle of answered prayer.

Willis straightened his glasses. "I never saw anything like that before," he uttered breathlessly.

Sandy was lifting a very scratched-up boy from the briar patch. Cecil shrieked as thorns resisted his rescue.

"Watch that there's no more snakes," Johnny warned.

"I don't think so," Sandy assured them as he held Cecil's hand coming up the steps. "The snake was probably just a loner checking out the food board."

Back at the log church, Cecil was in for an even more painful ordeal. One by one, Sandy extracted with a tweezer, every thorn that had stuck in the boy's legs, arm, and face. Then he sprayed on disinfectant, which made the stinging worse for a moment. Sandy comforted him in a quiet voice as big tears escaped Cecil's tightly closed eyes, smarting his cheeks.

The other boys left them to get the campsite cleaned up.

"Like always," commented Willis, "Cecil had to stir up more trouble than was needed."

Johnny nodded, but couldn't stop thinking that he would have been responsible if a tragedy had occurred because of his silence. And in this case, it could have.

"I know Cecil deserves to be punished," Scott said, "but I guess he's suffered enough. He's lucky someone like Sandy was here. Sandy's so good. He didn't even scold him."

"It's Charley that Cecil needs to thank," Willis declared. "And I-I'll be the one to catch it when I get home!" His lips trembled as his dark eyes moistened under the big glasses. "That is, *if* I g-get home."

Johnny went over and put an arm around the boy. "Don't you fret, Willis. Sandy'll get you there soon enough."

In a few minutes, everyone piled into the yellow station wagon and were homeward bound.

That night, Johnny wrote in his log book how Charley had come back and proved himself to be a real hero. After Sandy corrected his grammar and spelling later, his last paragraphs read:

> I told Aunt Lou all about Charley since we first found him. She said she never thought she'd be thankful for a pesky old chicken hawk, but she was glad for this one. I didn't let on how Charley was just doing what came natural to him. I reckon Aunt Lou hates rattlesnakes worse than she ever hated hawks.
>
> I've got a powerful respect for snakes, especially rattlesnakes. But I don't think you could say that I actually *hate* any critters.

13
Showdown

The school year was in its last two weeks, and Miss Blair's classroom stirred with restless boys and girls. Final tests were being held to see who was ready to be promoted.

Because so many exciting things had been happening on the mountain, Johnny had skipped lightly over his school work. Now panic began to set in.

In the log, he wrote:

May 27: Charley hasn't come to meet me for a week. I let the rats go, so I wouldn't have to keep feeding them. I'm glad to be through with that. I miss Charley, but I've got to get out of third grade. I'm twelve years old and three years behind already.

Louise had worked steadily all year. She was well prepared for tests, and agreed to help her brother. The night before the big spelling test, she called out words to him.

"I don't see why I need all this to be a conservationist," he complained.

"Sandy won't always be around to correct the records you keep," she said. "Don't forget. Anything you don't have to work for, isn't worth having—except salvation."

His mouth clamped into a tight, long line. Louise was so proper and right. She hardly ever sounded like a mountain person anymore when she talked.

At school, Cecil and Willis entertained the class with elaborate accounts of their runaway escapade. Each time, Cecil's version of the briar patch episode grew more spectacular. At the rate the snake increased in size, Cecil would soon be describing a giant anaconda.

"I launched the hang glider I made myself," he bragged. "If the severe turbulence off that high cliff hadn't caught me, there's no telling how high I would've soared."

Johnny scanned the faces of the children and exchanged knowing glances with Scott and Willis. Surely, even Cecil could see that no one believed him.

One good thing did seem to have come out of the incident: Cecil's parents had finally agreed on a plan for him to visit both of them.

"He's spending the summer in Asheville with his

Aunt Helen and Uncle Bill," Scott told Johnny. "They love children, but my mother says they don't put up with nonsense."

Perhaps there was hope for Cecil, after all. For the time being, however, Cecil the Pest was going full tilt. His foot in the aisle had to be coped with along with the unflattering remarks he regularly made. But for once, Johnny was surprised that he didn't mind.

Willis, however, no longer tagged after Cecil, humoring his every whim. "My parents understood I couldn't let him go off alone," Willis told Johnny, "but they said I should've called them before we got away from phones. Dad said he trusted me not to do something real stupid." He leaned toward Johnny, his dark eyes like buttons that almost filled up the thick lenses of his glasses. "But what about the Hermiteers? I mean—could I still visit on the mountain?"

"Sure," Johnny said. He almost slipped and added, "'specially since Cecil won't be around for awhile," but he didn't say it.

When the last day of school arrived, Johnny couldn't believe his final report card. He passed everything, and didn't even receive one "D." The cramming had paid off, but Sandy's tutoring had helped most of all.

Miss Blair looked pretty in her lavender dress. "I especially liked the paragraph you wrote on 'What I Want to Be,'" she told Johnny. "Conservationists are needed to keep the natural world the way it should be."

"I'm glad you let us use our dictionaries," he said, beaming.

"You've made real progress. I've recommended you for fifth grade math and science, even if you are promoted only to fourth grade."

"That makes me want to bust right through that ceiling up there," he exclaimed, smiling from ear to ear.

"Please don't," she laughed. "It's all I can do to keep this class from exploding before the bell rings!"

To celebrate school promotions, Ma fried a chicken to go with the tasty potato salad she'd made for supper. Aunt Lou brought a yummy caramel cake to go with a churn of homemade, vanilla ice-cream. Johnny noticed that his parents seemed to be getting along just fine.

Sandy had moved to the college dorm for the summer. When he brought the children home from school, he told them how good he felt about their promotions. Then he left to return the yellow station wagon to the school maintenance yard for the summer.

"How will you get to church services?" asked Louise.

"That's one for our prayer list," Sandy answered. "But believe me, I will get there somehow!"

After supper, Johnny went with Pa to check on his beegums under the sourwood tree.

"Pa," Johnny said, "it's not hawks that's stealin' Aunt Lou's chickens." Then he told his father what he had discovered at the rock plateau, and about the figure that had been seen on Top Trail more than once.

"When we mentioned it to Aunt Lou, she seemed real strange and told me and Ray Arthur not to tell anybody," he finished.

"What pushed you to it now, Son?" Pa asked as they walked back to the house.

Johnny paused. "Worryin' about Aunt Lou, I guess. I'd feel it was my fault if somebody did somethin' terrible to her. I couldn't stand that."

"You done right, tellin' me now. Your Aunt Lou's a tough one, but things ain't like they once was, with all sorts of criminals and dope addicts wanderin' 'round. We can't let her stay by herself, knowin' somebody's goin' in that yard of hers. I'll talk to her."

Johnny was quiet for a while. He didn't think Aunt Lou would listen to Pa, but what could he say? Finally, he said, "I don't think that'll work, Pa. Both you and Aunt Lou are about as stubborn as they come. Remember when you didn't give Ma a chance to talk you out of hang gliding lessons? Well, I doubt that Aunt Lou will let us look out for her any better. But I got an idea. I just need you standin' by me. Okay?"

Pa looked surprised. Then he said, "You got it."

When the women came out, Pa played the guitar for a good, old-time, family sing-along. Everything seemed so right.

Finally, Aunt Lou yawned and got up from the rocking chair someone had moved outside for her. "It's way past my bedtime," she announced. When she snapped her fingers, Midnight roused and stretched lazily.

"Wait, Aunt Lou," said Johnny, picking up the sack he'd packed his things in. "I'm goin' with you."

In the dim lantern light, she gave him a puzzled look. "That ain't necessary. I got Midnight."

Bracing himself for a storm that he was sure would come, Johnny took a deep breath. "I know you got Midnight. But you also got *me.* It ain't—isn't fittin' for you to be by yourself when we know somebody's stealin' your chickens."

She tried to fix him with one of her sternest glances and opened her mouth for a snappy comeback. He blocked it and went right on talking. "You're probably figurin' that I told Pa. And you're right. I did. I should've done it sooner. There's times when it ain't right to keep things from those who care about you." He sucked in a gulp of night air.

Ma and Louise looked on, amazed. Pa set down his guitar and listened in a new way.

"I'm sleepin' at your house, Aunt Lou," he said, "startin' tonight. I won't have it no other way!"

"*Any* other way," corrected Louise, absently.

"Whatever," Johnny finished, locking his arms around the bag against his chest.

For a full ten seconds, the boy and little old woman glared at each other. Then Aunt Lou looked at Pa.

Pa's arms were folded, too; his face was set in a stubborn mold. "It's either him or me that's gonna sleep in your spare room. But I snore real loud. You better take Johnny while you got the chance."

Aunt Lou breathed deeply, still glancing from father to son. Then her shoulders sagged a little. "Reckon I'll take the lesser of two evils. Let's go," she said to Johnny. "I do declare, you're showin' more Finlay guts every day, but I hope you still sleep quiet."

14
The Ghost Pays a Visit

On the first Saturday of summer vacation, Johnny woke early. Plans for the day had already had been made: Mr. Jenkins was going to drive Scott and Willis up to Aunt Lou's. The boys had agreed to weed her flower beds before going to hunt arrowheads.

Snuggled in the softness of a thick feather mattress, Johnny's body felt secure as a moth in its cocoon. Uneasy feelings had no place in him today, but one suddenly jabbed his consciousness.

The cabin was too quiet. He'd discovered that his great aunt snored louder than Pa, but the familiar rumble was missing.

The sharp crack of a rifle caused Johnny to pop out of bed like a jack-in-the-box.

"Aunt Lou!" he screamed as he sprinted through the back door and straight toward the chicken yard.

He had to skid to keep from knocking Aunt Lou down. She had the .22 rifle, but wasn't looking up where it was pointed. Midnight sat whining between her and whoever was at the gate.

"Horatio Tweed," she snorted, "Your poor ma, rest her soul, would turn over in her grave to know you was stealin'. You're lucky I shot up in the air!"

"Please, Miz Lou," a scratchy voice pleaded. "I didn't mean no harm. I was just sharin' your good fortune."

"You . . . you're a disgrace to good mountain people. You was a'stealin'! But this time, I'm gonna make you honest. Ain't nobody ever taught you to work for your vittles?"

"No, Ma'am. Folks has mostly treated me kindly."

Aunt Lou turned to Johnny, who was standing there staring at the old man who faced his great aunt. "Some kind of protectors you are; you in your underwear and Midnight just standin' there a'whinin'." She pointed to the man. "This here is Horatio Tweed, better known in town as 'Horace.' I come out here and found him holdin' a fryin'-sized pullet."

She turned to Horace. "This half-naked young'un's my great nephew. He was born and raised on this here mountain like your ma tried to raise you, Horatio. Your ma never run from work. She was a good, God-fearin' woman."

Horace looked ashamed, holding a warped felt hat in his hands. His dirty brown hair seemed to stand straight out all over. Edges of newspaper peeped from shirt sleeves and big floppy pants. He definitely had on more than one layer of clothes. His baggy trousers hung from a makeshift rag of a suspender that crossed his shoulder. At his ankles, they were tied with dingy strings. Several thicknesses of wool socks lay loosely over the tops of well-worn shoes.

Johnny caught a whiff of something foul. Cecil had been right. Horace needed a bath.

If the old man had grown up on the mountain, then he surely must know every path and hollow. There was no doubt in Johnny's mind that this was the ghost of Top Trail. It wasn't Hermit Dan. It was Horace, Cougarville's well-known bum. And unlike Hermit Dan, Horace was very much alive.

Some time later, when Scott and Willis arrived, Johnny was waiting out front. "C'mon," he beckoned, "and see the ghost!"

With puzzled looks, they followed him to the backyard.

"Mr. Horace!" cried Scott and Willis in unison. The old man sat on the back steps, spooning up grits and ham and eggs with gusto. At his feet, Midnight waited for any scraps that might fall.

"Mornin', boys." The old man's smile displayed one glittering gold tooth. "Miz Lou sure cooks up good vittles for a hungry workin' man," he told them.

"I didn't know you worked," Willis said.

"Well, I don't, generally." He nodded toward the kitchen. "But she made me work!" Horace paused to relish the last mouthful of grits and ham. He washed it down with milk from a pint jar, then swabbed off his mouth and unkempt beard with his shirt sleeve.

"I tell you no lie," he said with a big sigh. "I just give Miz Lou the cleanest chicken yard and cow stall on this here mountain." His face was bright with pride.

"It better be," Aunt Lou called from inside.

The boys giggled as she reached through the crack in the door for his empty plate.

"Much obliged, Ma' am," Horace said. "That's the best meal I had in a long time."

"There's always a good meal waitin' for them that's willin' to earn it, Horatio," she told him. "But I just better never catch you in my chicken yard again . . . less'n, of course, I send you there."

"No way, Miz Lou. I'll come to your door like you said."

The screen door popped open again. "Here's some biscuits for your back pack." She handed him a fat, brown bag. "There's a nice spring 'cross the road," she added, "where you can wash up before you start down the mountain." She coughed and turned her head to one side. "I wrapped a hunk of homemade soap in newspaper on top."

He thanked her again and tipped his hat. "I'm goin' now," he announced.

Midnight rose to follow, but halted quickly at Johnny's command. "Some watchdog you turned out to be," he said as Horace got out of hearing distance, "aidin' and a'bettin' a chicken thief."

"Midnight's an accessory to the crime," Scott chortled.

"Do you think Horace'll use that soap?" Willis wondered.

"Nope," Scott giggled. "He'll stuff the paper in his clothes and shoes. But take a bath? That might be hazardous to his health." The boys fell over each other as their merry laughter grew louder.

"You boys cut that out," Aunt Lou called from the kitchen. "Horace came from good, plain mountain stock. His head was just strung together different. Now he don't know no way but his own. The good Lord must've put the Horaces here for some reason." She paused. "Maybe t'was to remind you boys to wash behind ears and under fingernails." She came out and marched the three boys to her front yard.

Johnny hated to weed Aunt Lou's flower beds. She stood over them every second to make sure they didn't mistake basil and marigold seedlings for weeds.

"I'd rather clean Bossy's stall," complained Johnny from his knees. "Wish you'd made Horace do this."

"And stand over him that long?" She snorted, wrinkling up her little nose. "Only Midnight could stay that close by him . . . that trifling dog!"

At the sound of his name, Midnight hung his head and slid on his belly toward her.

"He's trying to say he's sorry," Scott observed.

"Well, Midnight or not, I don't think Horace'll sneak into this yard again," Johnny declared.

But it could have been someone worse, he thought.

It could have been someone who might have hurt his great aunt. He hadn't been anymore help than Midnight, but Johnny was glad he had insisted on being there, trying.

"I hear somethin' coming up the mountain," Willis said, cocking his round head to one side. The growl of a motor grew louder.

They had just finished working and were sipping grape soda on the porch when a faded blue four-wheel-drive station wagon pulled into view.

"Good gracious, it's Pa!" Johnny exclaimed as the driver waved. Across the top of the station wagon, wrapped in canvas, was something long and slender. Then Matt Bryan's head stuck out of the window as he beckoned them to follow them.

"Curlin' rattlesnakes!" Johnny bellowed as the car crept slowly up the mountain road. "Pa's gonna jump from Mirror Rock!"

15
Pa's Great Flight

"Well, don't wait for me," Aunt Lou ordered as they set down their cups. "I'm an old woman. If that fool nephew of mine gets himself killed, it won't be that long till I'll see him again, anyhow. I'll walk fast."

When the boys ran past the Finlay house, Ma had just come out with a basket of clothes to hang. Johnny yelled to her, and she called Louise. She didn't even take time to remove her apron with the big front pocket full of clothespins. As she bounded up the road, pins shook out of the pocket, dotting the road on both sides of her.

The blue station wagon was parked at Mirror Rock, but no one was there, and the hang glider was missing.

"Where is he?" panted Ma anxiously as she and

Louise caught up. "Has he done it yet?"

The boys looked off the rock. They looked below the rock.

"There's no sign of anything out there," informed Scott. "Not even a hawk."

When Scott said "hawk," Johnny remembered watching Charley soar over the east meadow in midmorning when the sun was at its brightest. "I think I know where they are," he cried, and led the way to Top Trail. "Follow me to the hermit hut!" he yelled.

Ma told Louise to wait for Aunt Lou so she'd know where to go. Seeing the state her mother was in, Louise didn't argue. It was plain, though, she wasn't thrilled over the prospect of being late for something like this.

Ma got there in time to see Pa strapped in the harness and perched like a grasshopper ready to jump off. Pa and Matt paid no attention as the onlookers came running up. Matt finished up the last-minute briefing. Then a gust of air came to meet them from the meadow. Pa's short legs could be seen stomping across the ledge. The big, pale green kite billowed above him.

"Here I go!" Pa called, and threw himself from the ledge. For a moment, Ma covered up her face. Pa was in the air and rising. Then something happened to the air currents, and he seemed to be going down instead of up.

"Oh, oh," squealed Willis. "Another Cecil in the briar patch!"

The boys ran to the edge of the cliff. Johnny's heart was pounding furiously.

"Please don't let him crunch," he prayed.

Aunt Lou and Louise arrived. Ma looked out at Pa and her face paled. The three women went together in a prayer huddle.

Matt was giving Pa instructions on a two-way radio. "Bank to the right," Johnny heard him say. Pa came down on the control bar and turned the kite. They watched him being lifted up, up, up into the blue-white sky till he steadied the craft just below a creamy white cloud.

Pa was airborne at last. Matt assured everyone that he was doing just fine and was no longer in danger. On the same current of air that his father was soaring on, Johnny now saw the bright orange-red glow of the tails of two hawks as they dipped and banked, free-riding.

"Well, I never!" Aunt Lou declared as she peered through her new spectacles. "To think I'd live to see a Finlay flyin' alongside chicken hawks."

"It is surely somethin' to see," Ma agreed. "That man of mine has got more guts than anyone I know!" There was honest-to-goodness admiration in her voice, and Johnny knew she wasn't fighting his father anymore.

Everyone marveled. Everyone cheered Pa's skillful handling of the glider as it drifted with ease and grace above the meadow.

Matt told them the landing place was near the road that snaked around the north side of the mountain.

Casey was waiting there in the Jeep to pick Pa up.

For more than thirty minutes, Pa floated through the air. Then he steered the craft toward the landing place. He touched down without stumbling.

"He's a natural," Matt declared. "Now we'll go get the Finlay station wagon and ride over, so I can load the kite onto my pickup.

Later, at the clearing beside the north road, Ma hugged Pa hard. "I'm proud of you," she murmured shyly, "and I'm sorry I gave you such a rough time about it. I was so scared, though. Losin' you would be like cuttin' off my right arm."

Pa's eyes got shiny with moisture. Johnny and Louise exchanged happy glances as their father said, "I'm sorry, too, Mae Beth. From now on, we're gonna talk over things like this, 'specially when we ain't agreein'. You wasn't wrong in what was frettin' you." He looked at Johnny and Louise. "A man's family has to be his first concern, after the Lord."

Matt and Casey Bryan waved from their pickup as they left for Cougarville.

"Aren't you still going to jump from Mirror Rock?" Louise wondered.

"Someday, maybe," Pa said, "but for a long time to come, my family comes first. I'm gonna work harder'n ever, so your dreams can come true!" He looked at the hawks as they still soared, silhouetted against the sky. "Like Louise's song goes," he added, "it's the wings the Lord puts in people's hearts that takes 'em the highest."

As their parents walked hand in hand to the station wagon, Johnny and Louise exchanged happy glances.

"Aunt Lou," Pa called back, "are you and them young'uns gonna stand there all day with your mouths open? Old Blue's a'waitin' to fly us home!"

"Old Blue?" Johnny questioned.

"My name for our new wheels," Pa explained.

Soon they were all singing Louise's song as they rode down the mountain road.